O' PENIEL,

BEHIND THE FANS

O'PENIEL,
BEHIND THE FANS
NO MORE COVER UPS

KIMBERLY WILLIAMS

iUniverse, Inc.
Bloomington

O' Peniel, Behind the Fans
No more cover ups

iUniverse books may be ordered through booksellers or by contacting:

iUniverse
1663 Liberty Drive
Bloomington, IN 47403
www.iuniverse.com
1-800-Authors (1-800-288-4677)

ISBN: 978-1-4759-7497-3 (sc)
ISBN: 978-1-4759-7498-0 (ebk)

Library of Congress Control Number: 2013901975

Printed in the United States of America

iUniverse rev. date: 02/20/2013

CHAPTER 1

The Opening of O'Peniel

O'PENIEL: Under the Fans

—No more cover-ups

Some say the angels in Heaven rejoice when babies are born or when the worldly become saved.

I, myself, believe in angels.

I see 'em being *full of glory* and *in praise* at all times.

Do they ever stop to take rest breaks from all of that singing?

Or, even stop to greet new members at those pearly gates?

Well, I sure believe in 'em.

I also believe we each have a guardian angel . . . and a death angel, too.

I pray every night that my guardian angel keeps continuous watch over me and strikes a deal each day with my death angel. Why? . . . So, that the death angel will keep postponing its visit.

I bet angels in Heaven look just like the ones on all of these church fans waving around in here.

Big wings, with clear eyes and silky, golden hair.

Nothing but music playing while they all fly around up there.

I wonder if they sing the same hymns we do down here on Earth.

Their flimsy clothes remind me of grandmommy's window coverings in her living room; light and airy—but, puffy when she catches a good breeze flowing through her house. So thin, though, their clothes seem to melt away just by looking at 'em.

"Mama, do angels have names?"

"Hush, *please*, Rhyah!" mama responds without even looking at me. Or, without the use of one of those fans. You see, every Sunday, church fans wave up. They wave down. During services, people constantly rock 'em back and forth like an 'ol lady rocking in a rocking chair. *"I wish I could just snatch 'em up. All of 'em. Or, make 'em vanish somehow,"* I say using my lower lip to blow my bangs off my sweating forehead. *"Yea, then what? What would come of these people with no fans to wave every Sunday morning? I'd love to know"*

It's so hot in church today that my under slip keeps sticking to my back, too.

I'm so bored!

I'm so hot!

Bored.

Hot!

About all I can do at this point is wish that Khoi, my younger brother, and I were still swimming at the city pool.

Mama doesn't allow us to swim that often, but she did take us yesterday.

She says all of that water has something in it that's not good for you.

"What it might be? I don't know. Don't have any idea."

It's not like we drink the pool's water. We only swim in it and sometimes have relay races.

Or, we'll dive to the bottom for quarters or chilled soda pop cans when the lifeguards decide to throw 'em in there.

I think she just doesn't want to have to do my hair afterwards.

I always feel fine after we go swimming.

But as for Khoi, he sometimes gets backaches and feels tired the next day. And sometimes the day after that.

He gets tired just like mama after he swims in a pool. I don't get it. Swimming is just like taking a long shower. So, why all the fuss? Mama, a person who rarely will go into details, just says the water is not good for us and never explains why. I know she loves my brother and I, but gosh! She worries about us too much. Stuff, that doesn't even seem to be a big deal to me. But, on the other hand, she's my mama;—and I guess it's a mama's job to worry about her kids.

Oh, mama's back and chest will hurt her at times, too. And by the way, she never swims. Never. I've never seen my mama even put her feet or legs in a pool.

Her arms and legs hurt her, too. They even swell. I've seen her in so much pain; she couldn't even go to work. She has told Khoi and I that she has strange shapes in her blood that look like little moons. These moons cause her to be tired a lot or even get real sick. So sick that she can barely walk. And like I said earlier—go to work.

She takes vitamins large enough to feed Uncle Sherman's horses. They're supposed to make her blood better.

Or, thicker.

Or, redder.

Or, something like that.

Her doctor makes her take 'em. These vitamins are light brown with dark, brown specks in 'em.

Bird eggs.

Yuk!

Yea, that's what they look like, a large container chalked full of bird eggs.

Still bored sitting here. "Mama, are you gonna always have to take those giant pills every morning?" I ask straightening my hair bow.

"*Be quiet*, Rhyah!" she quickly says attempting to quiet all of the sometimes unusual and often wild thoughts that constantly invade my head.

"But?"

"*Hush-up*! Don't you hear Rev. Reeves still preaching?

Now pay attention!" she tells me at once. Then, gives me one of her tight-eyed looks that always end with a slow roll of her neck and head.

All Rev. Reeves does is scream anyway, huh. I get sick of seeing and listening to this every Sunday! Yep. That's right. Every Sunday, he acts like no one can hear him unless he's yelling to the top of his lungs. He screams so loud while preaching that Heaven probably has to shut its doors for some quiet time.

Oh, how my mind continues to wonder while sitting in this church house . . . And something else . . . Did you know that my whole family goes to this church and has been since its existence.

Plus, . . . umm . . . about 40 or so other members from around town and other surrounding villages. Mama calls these surrounding areas communities, but our state maps call them um . . . ummm . . . un . . . unincor . . . unincorporated villages.

Oh, yea, O'Peniel, our church's name, was given by my grandfather, Papa Joseph.

He was grandmommy's husband and this church's first pastor. He's dead now.

Papa Joseph's strong hands helped build this small, white, wood-framed church that sits outside of town in a rural, un . . . unin . . . unincorporated area called Granville. The rear of the church needs a good touch-up, though. Its paint is starting to peel-off back there. You can tell, too. The sun rises upon the church's backside every Sunday morning. As the sun rises, it must hurt the paint because if you touch it, it'll smear onto your hands. Then, the paint will crack. Then, it falls to the ground leaving only the Cypress wood to show.

O'Peniel is located out in the country—right off a red dirt road that's lined with pine trees.

Giant pine trees, I'd say. Or, gigantic Christmas trees—whichever way you want to see 'em as. Every now and then, you'll catch a glimpse of a Magnolia tree; especially, when their in full bloom.

Other than that, O'Peniel's not too far from the shallowest end of the Le Tulle Swamp.

The church's foyer barely exceeds the size of mama's walk-in closet at home.

Its sanctuary comfortably seats all members. Just about everyone in here sits in the same spot every Sunday anyway, though.

The ol' marquee' standing in front of the church reads: O'Peniel Missionary Baptist Church along its top. The marquee' got turned a little due to a hurricane that came through about two years ago. I noticed that the sign had changed and swiveled around a bit. Mama said that she hadn't noticed it. Grandmommy said that as long as God knows where to come, it was ok. Each Sunday, Rev. Reeves' sermon topic is always put up there. He'll do his very best to place each Sunday's sermon topic up there even if it's missing a few letters.

It's funny to me how O'Peniel got the name that we call it today. The letter 'O' was placed in front of the word "Peniel" because visitors used to have trouble trying to locate this church; being that it's out here in the country and all.

But, more so, because on mornings before heavy fog had begun to lift, people would have to stop and flag down other drivers for directions.

Some people, however, would get their directions from the owner of a farmhouse that's located at the point where the black top ends and the dirt road begins leading right up to our church.

Otherwise, people who knew where our church was located would answer "OH! Peniel!" and simply give its directions.

Somehow . . . and over the years, the letter 'H' in the word 'OH' got dropped and it's been known as 'O'Peniel' every since.

But, before all of this, our church's original name was Peniel Missionary Baptist Church.

Mama told me that the word "Peniel", by itself, meant *"coming face to face with God"*.

Brown, high-back, wooden benches are placed in rows to make up our pews.

The choir stand contains only two, short rows of fold-up chairs. Their rickety, so the choir has to stay situated when seated for long periods of time. Rev. Reeves' sermon is a good example of having to stay seated for loooong periods of time.

A boring time, too.

During this time, I use it to think about other stuff.

Stuff like: school and my friends. Or, other stuff.

Anyway, the only carpet in the church is in the tiny pulpit area where Rev. Reeves is standing.

It's red and all worn down. Just like those chairs up there in the choir stand.

All summer long, big box fans push the hot air out of here.

When it's cold, the deacons light gas heaters for us. The heaters are old, too. Half the time, we'll get more gas floating around in here than heat.

Waving around, back and forth up in here are O'Peniel's trademarks.

Church fans.

Uh ha, church fans.

I call 'em trademarks because they're always visible. Plus, I learned in school that a trademark was something that symbolizes something or that stands for something.

Or, something like that.

They're always readily available, too.

Members will pick these fans up before they will their own bibles.

When Papa Joseph was preaching here, these hand fans were used only during the summertime. Now, they wave around all year long, whether it's hot or cold outside.

After Papa Joseph died, Rev. Reeves took over preaching and has been screaming and beating at that pulpit every since. That's why the pulpit now leans a bit at the top along with scratches and stuff. It leans real good to his right and to the congregation's left. I see it now—leaning as he uses it to help sturdy himself while yelling. I wonder if his bible has ever slowly moved to the right on its own.

Anyhow, he carries a big, thick, black bible with gold trim. On the cover, it has engraved letters that you can barely read.

He uses it to beat on that pulpit when trying to *deliver* a secret message to *someone*—out loud.

Or, to make a *blown-up* 'holy' point about *something*.

That's why his bible's edges appear roughed-over and its pages are frazzled.

Rev. Reeves is a tall man with pointy shoulders and long, stretchy arms.

He's as dark as the sun's shadow on a clear, summer day.

"Yes, a day just like today", I say to myself glancing over a few heads out a window.

His eyeglasses are what really get under my skin, though. Small, oval-shaped lenses with a silver border—too little for his face if you ask me—but mostly, those glasses are just another tool he uses to search out his victims.

I think he's too young to be a preacher.

Huh!

Maybe this is why I think he's so strange.

All the preachers I know are old with big tummies.

Old and fat men.

Not young ones.

Men with grandkids, like Khoi and I.

Tall and skinny is what he is. Those lanky legs remind you of a person using chopsticks.

He speaks and preaches with a heavy voice that'll make a baby cry for its mama; if his thick beard doesn't scare the baby first!

"Thunder!"

Yeeeaaaa!

Ah ha! That's what his deep, raspy voice sounds like alright! But, how can a man so slim have such a cold and harsh sounding voice?

"Mama, do you think Rev. Reeves' voice echoes like thunder?" I ask, knowing I am about to draw the line this time.

Mama pretends to ignore me, but I know that she hears me by the way she sits there and twitches her body immediately before sighing to herself.

First, mama twists her upper body to her left side.

Afterwards, she gives a harder twitch to the right that leads to an exhale of it all.

It begins in her stomach, raises-up into her chest, clears in her throat and ends through the nose.

I wait a moment to make out whether she'll reply.

Nothing.

Not O-N-E reaction . . .

And the only sound I hear is that of air being slowly released through her nostrils; like air escaping out of an airtight balloon.

Watching her inflated chest go flat again, I probe for a second time, "Mama, does Rev. Reeves' voice sound harsh to you?"

Mama still does not answer.

Interrupted yet again by my inattentiveness, she seems to add to her usual methods of being irritated. She rearranges her feet on the floor, quickly snaps her neck and head back, sharply twists to both sides, and then slowly breathes out.

Even with me obviously staring at her, she still does not give-in.

Firm and steadfast is her appearance.

. . . . Just simply unwilling to bulge.

Realizing that I've pushed way too far, I too, turn to listen to Rev. Reeves continue his fiery sermon.

"We all know of the Father, but have we all really found Him!" he jolts at the congregation.

"Be washed in His blood and stay close to His commandments!" Rev. Reeves continues to say.

Sweat rolls down his forehead.

This causes his glasses to trickle down his nose.

Rev. Reeves pauses.

He pats the back of his neck with his wrinkled handkerchief.

"Find Him again and keep Him near this time!" he blows while banging his bible against any corner of the pulpit.

The pulpit rocks with each consistent beat.

Sweat continues to develop; only for it to leave his forehead and run-down his shadowy neck.

For the moment, his handkerchief lay crushed inside his hand; very tightly smothered within his grasp.

"Don't hold back. Return to His 'fold' at once!" he raves toward the pews.

Church members remain quiet.

So do I while looking near Jesus' portrait for anything noticeably 'folded' in it or around it.

Confused, I turn away to look up at mama. I notice she's quiet, too.

"Is she trying to figure out what a 'fold' could be like I am?

I don't know . . ." At this point, I can only presume not wanting to bother her right now.

Hand fans are raised as Rev. Reeves goes on to continue with his ravaging outbursts.

This is the tone that always comes right before he seizes his victim for the day.

A 'holy hush' is what I call it when moments like these occur.

Ya know—kinda like 'the calm before the storm'.

Seeing this reminds me of the day Khoi and I were baptized over there in that swamp.

He preached so hard and prayed so long that misty morning . . . till I thought I was going to drown; all while he had me submerged under that murky water. After our baptism, Khoi and I stood there shaking while Rev. Reeves continued to shout out loud about us now being God's children.

By what I've overheard from mama, Rev. Reeves has never been married.

He moved to the South immediately after being 'called to preach'.

He doesn't have any children, but tries to participate in all civic activities around town; whether the activities are for children or being held for grown folks.

What gets me, though! He'll even attend activities that he wasn't invited to.

He's bossy, too. Yep, he sure is. Aunt Gayla told Grandmommy and Grandmommy told mama that he had that red dirt laid over the regular dirt road leading to the church so that it would not kick up so much. That red dirt is supposed to have clay in it so that when it hardens, it would be more like the black top road. Aunt Gayla was right when she told Grandmommy that that was a waste of the church's building fund money.

Well, as you guessed . . . that red dirt kicks up, too. Especially, in the summer time. On a day like today those temporary, little dust storms will follow people as they drive till they reach the black top. Now, instead of the dust storms only being kinda gray-like or even white, they're red.

Weird!

He is plenty weird and as strange as his clothes and ways.

Rev. Reeves refuses to wear a pastor's robe.

Ya' know, one of those robes that look sorta like the kind our choir members are wearing up there. He announced when he first visited O'Peniel that during all of his sermons, he wanted the congregation to know who he was and what he represented without covering it all up. Like today and as always, I've only seen him dressed in all-black for his Sunday sermons. Or, while he's out and about in town as far as that goes.

Black pants.

Black shirts that mostly button up to the neck.

Never a tie.

And the same ol' black shoes that he's been wearing since he first visited here.

The shoes' soles always leave smudge marks on our church's wooden floors.

Rev. Reeves was picked over two other visiting pastors that looked like *regular* pastors to me; they were both old and had families already. One of 'em even had a lot of grand-children around the same age as Khoi and I. I don't know why, but neither of the other preachers was asked to return for a second visit. O'Peniel only ended up inviting Rev. Reeves to return for a second time to preach.

I remember: The Sunday following his second visit, O'Peniel's deacons stood before the church and announced Rev. Reeves would be our next pastor.

Today is the last Sunday of the month.

So, I know services are going to be long. Well, *long-winded* is what I really want to say.

On most Sunday mornings, I ride with mama to church. Khoi always rides with Uncle Sherman. Neither of us ever want to ride with Aunt Gayla. She likes to hear us go over bible verses. But worse, sometimes we'll have to give her a rundown of what happened at school the past week.

Aunt Gayla is mama's only sister and Uncle Sherman is her only brother.

Mama's the oldest. Uncle Sherman is the youngest of grandmommy's children. Aunt Gayla is in the middle and has no kids. Since Khoi and I are not hers, I don't know what gives her the right to always quiz us.

Moreover, she's real picky.

Just plain picky about everything-

Picky about her clothes. Picky about her car. And even picky about her house.

Picky about how my brother and I act or speak in public.

Who really cares!—Is what I'd like to tell her one day!

This is probably why she hasn't married yet. No man wants a finicky wife who's always analyzing everything.

She's even picky about her food. Different types of foods can't touch on her plate.

She doesn't want anything on her plate to run together, either.

If her foods do any of this, she can't eat 'em!

Yep! Those foods will just be left separate and uneaten.

If there's something she's eating like: mustard greens and its pot liquor begins to run by some of her meat, she'll immediately get a napkin to sop-up the extra juice.

Or, she'll fold a napkin like a professional dry cleaner, placing it neatly in between her foods to section everything off.

It's just as simple as that!

"Is Aunt Gayla ever going to get married or have kids, mama?" I begin to explore forgetting about her previous warnings.

"I! Do! Not! Know!" mama snaps.

Then, she looks away; focusing on my brother making paper airplanes out of today's church programs.

Out of the corner of my mouth, ". . . . because Auntie Gayla's too picky, huh, mama? Huh?" I say again to her surprise.

At that moment, she turns her head further away from me; smiling while trying to hold back her laughter.

Khoi is so lucky. He gets to sit in church with his friends or by my step-cousins near Uncle Sherman while I have to always sit here by mama as if I were posing for a picture.

Perfectly poised, I have to always sit.

My legs; they must be closed or crossed.

Just look at that—I see Khoi 'cuttin'-up' again—right now. He's passing paper airplanes back and forth to Uncle Sherman's step kids and then onto some other boys.

They play before church service . . . during service . . . and again after service.

Khoi, Uncle Sherman's step kids, along with those other boys really cut-up when Bro. Campbell, a blind deacon, falls asleep in church. They make fun of the way he grips his cane while nodding off . . . and they won't stop unless my Uncle Sherman decides to separate 'em onto other pews. One time, mama had to send a note to Khoi through the hands of four church members to tell him to stop acting-up so much in church. Khoi read the note, but when he felt it was all clear, he resumed mimicking Bro. Campbell.

Bro. Campbell bobs his head up and down when he's 'napping' in church; only waking up to say 'amen' and then nodding back off again.

Even when there's no preaching or praying going on, he'll still say 'amen' . . .

When the collection plate reaches him, he'll say 'amen' instead of putting money in it . . . When the choir is singing, he hums 'amen' instead of singing the real words . . .

Asleep and unaware, Bro. Campbell will eventually looses the grip on his black cane.

When this happens, the cane will then slip, crash to the floor; and make a clattering sound before it settles on the floor.

'Clank', 'clank', 'clunk' are the rhythmic sounds that cane makes nearly every Sunday during these long sermons.

This noise always catches people off-guard because it echoes throughout these Cypress wood floors. I'm shocked today that his cane has not already hit the floor being that he's bobbing his head right now . . . asleep with that cane barely fastened within his grasp.

Using a hand fan, grandmommy waves over her left shoulder in order to get mama's attention. After doing so, grandmommy, with tension in her eyes, slightly tilts her head to glare straight at me. She subsequently hints to mama that I'm daydreaming yet again. (Mama, a long time ago, probably developed these same sorta looks from grandmommy as a child.)

Instantly, mama elbows a rib on my right side.

"Rhyah, what are you staring at over there?"

"Nothing," I instantly reply, not wanting her to know that I was watching Bro. Campbell sleep . . . AND waiting for that cane to slip.

Then mama, herself, begins to stare at him; just the same.

With Rev. Reeves always blaring in here, I still can't figure out how Bro. Campbell is able to nod-off like that.

Besides being blind, Bro. Campbell is one of our four deacons. He sits on the side of the church as does the other deacons during church services; but just doesn't actively participate as one. He's probably our oldest member at O'Peniel.

I know.

How? . . . because there's a rusty, wall plaque mounted near the front of the church which has his name engraved in it. His name appears on the plaque as does Papa Joseph's name.

And some other men whom mama says have all died.

"Mama, what time is it?"

Conscious that I am going to continue to get on her nerves, she bends down to fidget with her stockings.

She rises back up to straighten a gold cross that's hanging loosely around her neck.

A long . . . and . . . deep breath is taken.

After all of this, she bends back down to fret a moment inside her purse.

Rising back up in agitation, mama pulls out a brand new pack of chewing gum and shoves it in my face.

"Here. Take two sticks of this and chew on them till church is over, *alright*!"

"Yes, mam," I carefully reply.

I know I have gotten on mama's nerves for certain now.

Especially, if she's going to allow me to chew gum in church.

Something a young lady should never do—as Aunt Gayla would put it.

Huh! I wish Rev. Reeves would stop yelling about people being delivered from their sins or staying in some type of 'fold' and 'flock'.

"What's a *fold* or *flock*, anyway?" I still wonder, but scared to disturb mama.

Doesn't he know people were born into this world. No one ever says we folded or flocked into this world. Or at least that's what I've been told. Whenever he begins to preach with a lot of gust or rumbling thunder, rest assure that someone is to become his next target.

He'll try to get a point over to *someone* in these pews. He does this every Sunday before stepping away from that pulpit. Most of the time, he'll do it with a frown upon his shiny face that'll out do one of mama's looks any day.

"Uh, oh!"

"Mama, why does Rev. Reeves keep looking over at Aunt Lorice every time he mentions the word—'*sinner*'?"

"*Girl*!" mama replies with no patience, "I am going to take you to the bathroom and beat your behind if you do not stop worrying me!

Now pay attention, Rhyah Ann!"

Mama's tone is low, but sharp.

Sharp: with a lot of force behind it.

This is the kind of pitch she uses when she puts her lips right up to your ear and pretends to only be whispering. But, the sound penetrates down into your ear canal very loud and clear.

"Renew your spirit and wash your soul clean! Rejoin the fold!

Don't follow the path you're on, but seek His path of righteousness!"

Rev. Reeves yells while pointing his bible in Aunt Lorice's direction.

Aunt Lorice is one of grandmommy's sisters. She and her husband divorced long before Khoi and I were born. She wears this lipstick that looks thick and creamy enough to be raspberry peanut butter. The make-up painted around her eyes is forever noticeable, even from great distances.

I've even caught her flipping through one of my hip-hop magazines titled 'What's Up, Girl!' admiring its clothes. She dresses in the same 'in style-fashions' that the magazine advertises. She buys skirts and church dresses in the petite-size section of stores so that they'll automatically stop above her knees.

As if she's shame, Aunt Lorice throws up her fan every time Rev. Reeves hollers, "Throw away your sinful ways!"

She has men from around town to do lots of things for her.

For some reason, most of these men are already married. I guess this is why mama never takes us over to her house. These men buy her groceries and wash her car on Saturdays, so that it is glossy and all set for Sunday mornings.

Bro. Carrington, our head deacon, once brought some freshly caught fish over to Aunt Lorice's house. He was cleaning 'em on her front porch when Mrs. Carrington drove up. She spun right up into the middle of Aunt Lorice's front yard.

Trails of mud tracks were left in her grass.

I found all this out by having overheard mama and Aunt Gayla talk.

Besides this, all I can remember is Aunt Lorice having to wear a cast on her left arm for months.

Mama gives me another nudge.

Then, lowers her head to whisper, "Stop all that daydreaming! Church is over," without even moving her lips. Afterwards, she gently massages both temples on each side of her face.

Thank goodness! Rev. Reeves has finally finished preaching! Sis. Bradley would have torn up that organ if he hadn't stopped when he did. He takes his seat to the right of pulpit with legs that are moving like the stilts circus clowns perform on.

Once seated, he angles his body to stare Aunt Lorice down in a cold-hearted way.

At last it's time for the final offering.

All of O'Peniel's deacons rise to collect the offering.

All except for Bro. Campbell, of course . . . He remains asleep.

Rev. Reeves sat down minutes ago.

Still appearing angry and passionless; he sits there gleaming over three pews at Aunt Lorice. Like a hawk ready to snatch its prey . . .

Well, . . . actually he's watching her church fan—because it's still plastered against her face.

The offering plate continues through the pews as I sit here wondering why people, especially grown-ups, hold these hand fans up to their faces like that. Or, for that matter, *have to have 'em* every Sunday morning.

Are these fans *really* being used to fan away the heat or *one's secrets or even their sins?*

I have seen people sit in these pews on Sundays mornings looking so holy.

But, when the following Monday comes, no one has any shame or forgiveness.

These flimsy, little things waving around in here don't give me any confidence.

What's the connection?

'Life' is not 'life' unless we 'live' it.

"Mistakes are going to find us along the way or at one point or another."

This is what Grandmommy always tells Khoi and I when we've made a bad grade or have gotten in trouble.

Besides, with mama and Auntie Gayla's eyes constantly on me, I dare not make too many mistakes. But, I do know that these church fans will *never ever* keep me from hiding behind my fears in life.

"Is that it?"

FEAR? I ask myself as the collection plate reaches the first hand of our pew.

What is there to be fearful of?

God has already basically instructed: *"Have no fear, for He is always with us!"*

"Here is a quarter, Rhyah," mama states interrupting my thoughts.

Using an open palm, she slides it over and then states, ". . . and give me those gum wrappers, too, please!"

The whole congregation is standing awaiting benediction. Well, that is everyone except for Aunt Lorice and Bro. Campbell. Bro. Campbell, being ol' and blind, never stands during any parts of our church services.

As for Aunt Lorice—she stays planted in her seat, peeking through those who stand in front of her—still shielding herself from Rev. Reeves.

CHAPTER 2

Fun and Play Time

Khoi and I have been playing outside all afternoon.

Mama has laid in her bed since returning home from church. We usually see her peeking through the screen door to check on us; hollering at Khoi and his friends for playing football on her grass; and let me not forget—telling me not to ride my bike past the corner.

But, not today.

As the evening draws on, he and I catch Lightening Bugs.

Khoi keeps trying to pull their tails off in order to see if they'll still glow.

Mama must not be feeling too well.

Because . . . well, she still has not come to the screen door all evening; not even to make us get ready for school tomorrow.

As I recall, I did see her readjusting her stockings several times during church this morning. Sitting in the same position for a while or wearing tight-fitting stuff (like panty hose) tends to limit the blood flow in her legs.

We prepared our own dinner plates earlier. Mama fried chicken wings for me and legs for Khoi before we left for church. She usually fusses at Khoi for only eating the skin and crust and not the meat, but not today. I guess she had more energy then than she does now. She always seems to have more energy in the mornings, anyway, though. She cooked a stock pot full of mustard greens yesterday. She removed all of those long, white stems from 'em, too. Khoi and I love eating greens; any kind basically, just without those stringy stems. And so, we ate chicken, greens with some sweet Atchafalaya cornbread.

Oh, yea; and don't let me forget the hot sauce. We just love hot sauce on our greens.

Yes, indeed. . . . and Louisiana Hot Sauce, at that.

All mama has had to eat since leaving church is a baked yam. She left its peels sitting in a plate on the kitchen counter—right next to all the other dishes that we've accumulated today. Mama keeps a lot of yams stocked in the bottom bin of our refrigerator. She eats at least two of 'em per week.

She'll wrap 'em tightly in foil.

Bake 'em till they're all mushy inside.

And then slit their tops for butter and brown sugar. They're supposed to help keep her healthy. And somehow do something for her blood. She'll only add other spices if she's serving 'em to my brother and I.

Mama always tucks us into bed. But, tonight's different.

Ya see, there's a routine she otherwise uses. It's called 'Hugs and Kisses Time' or 'Kisses and Hugs Time'. Either way you wanna say it is o.k.

But, it's her special bedtime ritual for us.

She takes turns as to who'll get theirs first. Mama used to sing to us, but I told her we were getting too old for that. So now, she only hugs and kisses us. Kissing us in a funny way that tickles our cheeks and necks.

How?

I'm tickled just thinking about it. She tucks us into bed. Then, she tucks-in both of her lips and gnaws as hard as she can on our necks and cheeks till we can't stop laughing. Afterwards, she hugs us with all of her might. Her strong hugs feel so good.

Before daddy left, it was more like 'Fun and Play Time.' We'd hide somewhere in our rooms and he'd pretend not to be able to find us.

Mama never approved of this during bedtime!

"Royce!" She'd yell from their bedroom, "They n-e-e-e-d to go to bed!" Daddy would always ignore mama and keep on playing with us.

One night, she surprised all three of us! Mama was tired of daddy ruining our bedtime, I guess. While daddy was giving us pony rides on his back, mama snuck outside and tapped on Khoi's window first and mine's next.

I remember her making ghost-like sounds outside both of our windows. She howled louder than the winds during hurricane season. This must be the reason Mrs. Thibodeaux' dog next door kept growling that night. That dog must have been scared, too.

Throwing her body around, mama even tried to act is if she was going to fly away as she appeared under the moonlight.

We did not know what to think. We all kept seeing this shadowy-figure waving its arms, among other things, but we definitely did not know it was her. Mama was acting like some sort of strange creature. The glow from the moon outlined her silhouette against our windows. She'd move her body about in bizarre ways first in front of Khoi's window and then she'd run to mine and do the same thing. Her bulky house robe made it seem as if there really was a ghost outside.

"Vanessa!" daddy initially yelled. "Nessa!" He yelled, again, in a rushed voice. The next time, he stretched his voice out to scream: "Va-n-e-s-a-a-a-a!" And as if that weren't enough, daddy called out to mama two more times as we three stood in the hall between me and Khoi's bedrooms.

Mama never answered, of course. Khoi was so alarmed, he ran into her bedroom; only to find her not in there. Panic stricken like in the movies is how he came bursting back out with a cry of horror breaking from his lips, "The ghost has eaten mama already!"

Daddy's eyes were bucked and his hands trembled as he pushed us closer toward him. With uncertainty in his voice, "What? She's not in there?" He promptly questioned Khoi. The way daddy's eyes had bulged-out made me that much more frightened.

Like Khoi, I was starting to think the ghost had already gotten mama, too.

"BANG!" Our patio door in the back had slammed shut.

My whole body jumped.

Daddy's eyes were jumping, too. That's when you bulge out your eyes hoping not to miss seeing anything, but your head never moves.

Khoi dropped to the floor, kneeling and praying aloud.

With his knees a'rattlin' and his body a'shakin', all I recall coming from his mouth that night was "Please, Oh, Please, Lord! . . . and I remember hearing him say *mama* a couple of times . . .

Khoi, scared to death, just slid right through most of the words in his prayer.

Then, we heard something else. . . . . "Shrishhhh!"

"Oh! This is so horrible!" I thought to myself at the time.

And there it was again! "Shrishhhh!" They were scratchy-type sounds scraping along another hallway from inside the house. "Daddy, it's gotten in the house." I remember telling him.

Khoi, still on both knees, began to pray again and even louder this time.

'It' was dragging against the walls making those scratching noises that seemed to be getting closer. Boldly, daddy attempted to edge around the corner in order to meet up with 'it' at once.

"Nooooo!" Khoi and I mustered to get out, both tugging onto daddy's shirt in order to hold him back.

"Boom!"

"Boom!"

"BOOM, BOOM!"

Suddenly, some loud pounding sounds began to vibrate along the walls. Mama was going out of her way to slam doors in other parts of the house. This made it seem as if 'it' was surely going to get us now.

"Another boom was heard coming our way. But not before a number of other loud bangs!"

All of this, followed-up by other long 'shrishhhh' sounds. It was mama still using a tree limb from outside and her open hand to slap hard against walls.

The noises got even closer and not to mention louder. And as *it* got closer, *it*, too, seemed to get louder. Khoi quickly rose up, smashing his face into daddy's stomach; not wanting to see what was about to approach us.

Daddy again tried to march forward.

But, couldn't!

Out of fear, Khoi had lodged his feet on top of daddy's feet and I wasn't about to let go of his belt loops. I remember Khoi only removing his smothered face long enough to holler, "Daddy, don't leave us!" before reburying it for a second time. Daddy held us tight as the creepy sounds penetrated around the corner.

I didn't know whether to look straight ahead like daddy was doing or to cover my face like Khoi.

At once, mama appeared from around the corner and stood there in front of us.

She raised her arms up in the same weird way as she'd done outside our windows letting us know it was her all the long.

She broke out laughing so hard, she cried after seeing our faces.

"N-o-o-o-o-w GO to s-l-e-e-e-e-p!" she commanded in that same howling voice.

I can still remember her laughing once she'd made it into their bedroom.

We all just stood there stunned.

Daddy: looking on at her in disbelief.

Me: not knowing what to say.

And Khoi: speechless; just chewing away on his pajama top.

She'd gotten us and she knew it! From that point on, unless it was the weekend, daddy no longer kept us up past our bedtimes. He'd otherwise only kneel down with my brother and I as we said our prayers.

And as far as mama was concerned, daddy's *'Fun and Play Time'* was over!

I miss all of that.

I miss his funny faces and I surely miss him playing around with us.

He liked to tease Khoi and I. Especially, when we had gotten in trouble about something with mama. He seemed to entertain us when we had gotten in trouble which always made our punishments seem a little lighter.

Those times were cool!

Yea, I miss him and him clowning around with my brother and I.

I wonder if daddy misses us, too.

Tonight, however, mama tells each one of us to pretend we were her and to take turns doing what she does before we go to bed. Mama then turns around without making eye contact. She heads toward her bedroom using the walls as an aid for every other step she takes.

After that, her bedroom light goes off before she slowly shuts her the door.

"Hey Rhyah, I've beat your score again on this video game. My initials are now firrrrst. My initials are firsttttt!"

Ha! Ha!" he again taunts from his bedroom.

I am trying to follow mama's ritual, but Khoi just wants to use this time to act as if we are home alone for the night.

"My—score—is—high—er! My—score—is—high—er!" he now chants from a distance, still playing that video game; knowing that mama would whip his behind if she caught him doing so.

CHAPTER 3

Trapped

The middle of next week has approached and mama still has that same sour look about her. This is the look that comes right before her eyes and fingernails turn a different color.

A funny-looking mustard color.

No, wait!—Creole Mustard.

Yea, that's what that golden brown shade resembles to me. It tastes good, too.

Pearly-white is how they appear when she's o.k. So, she is not so bad off right now because her nails are all still pearly white.

Grandmommy and Aunt Gayla call if they are not over here visiting us or to check on mama. Mama goes to work, but has gotten off early just about every day so far; seeking only her bed as soon as she gets out of her car. Khoi continues pestering mama about going swimming again.

She has told him 'No!' so many times that Aunt Gayla had to interrupt yesterday and scold him on the number of times he'd already bothered mama about going.

Khoi knew not to give Aunt Gayla any 'lip service', so he only mumbled under his breath and went into his bedroom.

Mama did receive a shot today. It's some type of shot that gives her energy and seems to keep her out of the bed as much. During these spells, we all know to be patient and wait for her condition to pass. Homework and TV are pretty much the only adventures that surround our home at times like these.

Another Saturday morning has happened upon us.

Today, Uncle Sherman comes by to pick up Khoi to go horseback riding in a pasture near his stable. His horse trailer and extended-cab pickup truck take up the whole curbside out front.

"Honk. Honnnk."

"YES! Uncle Sherman's here!" Khoi remarks, hopping around in a circle trying to put on his other boot. Uncle Sherman gets out of his truck, but reaches back-in to get his cowboy hat. The truck's heavy duty engine remains running. If I did not know any better, I'd think there as an 18-wheeler parked outside the house.

His long legs and slender body race up our sidewalk wearing an outfit geared for a rodeo.

"I barely heard your horn over that diesel engine." Mama tells Uncle Sherman while letting him inside.

Khoi enjoys doing whatever Uncle Sherman finds interesting.

Horseback riding, rodeos, hanging out—just doing whatever.

Uncle Sherman's step-sons remain in the truck peeking through a rear-side window.

I notice 'em while peeping over Uncle Sherman's shoulder as he gives me a hug. Uncle Sherman's hugs seem to require so much effort on his part. First, Uncle Sherman has to separate both legs. He, then, has to bend his knees after pulling up his front jean pockets. His long back stretches down toward me like a see-saw. Finally, he'll push my head toward his. Being so tall, I guess he has to complete these steps in order to reach me.

Grandmommy, along with Aunt Gayla, arrive shortly after Uncle Sherman does.

His step-sons are still watching every move concerning this house. They even watch Grandmommy and Aunt Gayla coming in, as well. It's like they're at a drive-in movie or something.

"Camel, are you ready?" he calls out to my brother.

Then, Uncle Sherman hugs mama the same way in which he always hugs me. He also reminds her to be thankful that last week's smaller crisis was not a 'full-blown' one.

Since his truck is still running, he does not hang around long.

"We're gone." Uncle Sherman states holding the door open for Khoi.

He then asks Khoi, "What position are you going to play in football this season?" My brother does not even reply. Excited, he simply runs out the door; so thrilled that he's finally able to spend some time away from this house. Uncle Sherman pulls off with Khoi waving good-bye as if he's in a parade—wearing only a big Mardi Gra smile with one hand waving over the other.

"I'll probably be stuck in this house all day." I sit in my room imagining.

I am not too happy about being trapped in here at first, but overhearing Grandmommy, Aunt Gayla and mama talk about recent events is going to make my day speed by just that much faster.

CHAPTER 4

The Better Deal

Mama is doing much better, but not well enough to go to church this Sunday morning, She is, at least, moving around much better than last week, though.

Grandmommy arrived at our house pretty much at the crack of dawn in order to help out. She actually did a lot more than helping out. She's already vacuumed and dusted the whole house while washing at least two loads of clothes.

After her cleaning spree, she made a huge breakfast that resembled a buffet-style set up. A set-up just like the ones on cruise ships. Either that or, one that's advertised in magazines from those big, fancy hotels.

She's even placed all of mama's fine china out on the table that she and daddy received when they married. The spoons and forks are neatly arranged within reaching distance from a whole platter full of bacon and fresh, pork sausage patties.

A growling sound escapes from the pit of my stomach.

I can't tell if it's because I smell the bacon or if it's because of the sausage.

Hot out of the frying pan, they both continue to sizzle on the china platter.

Eager to please, "Help yourselves. Over there are the scrambled eggs and hard boiled ones, too, kids." Grandmommy, then, points to every other item on the kitchen table, making sure that we don't overlook anything. I skip over the eggs and French toast, to head for her homemade buttermilk biscuits. Grandmommy's biscuits are big and thick and always come out with a light brown crust. She melts extra butter to put on their tops even though everyone always breaks them apart to put extra butter on the insides. Uncle Sherman loves her biscuits as much as I do. We both like to dip 'em in her homemade sugar-syrup.

Mama, wrapped in her thick robe, strolls into the kitchen. She retrieves a glass out of the cabinet. "It smells good in here," she mentions before drawing a deep breath to pop one of those horse pills into her mouth. Then, chases it down with a tall glass of tap water.

Khoi hastily lays his crowded plate down in order to reach for a bowl. Impulsive as ever, he nearly scalds his wrist when his sleeve dips into the gravy boat which holds the steamin' sugar syrup.

Using a napkin to dab at his wrist and sleeve, "What's that?" he asks with gaping eyes.

We notice grandmommy is placing a covered container onto the table.

"I'm sorry ya'll. I'd almost forgotten this from inside the refrigerator.

It's Fresh Fruit Medley. I even drizzled a little honey over it for you, Rhyah."

Khoi is so excited about our buffet-style breakfast that he kisses Grandmommy on both cheeks. Like Khoi, I needed a bowl, too, but not for the fresh fruit. Mine was for her grits. She makes the best grits and I like mine swimming in butter! Her grits are always perfect because she adds a little sugar to the pot.

Mama and Grandmommy ate after we did. I noticed our plates were heftier than theirs.

"By the time Gayla Marie arrives, there will still be plenty left over for her,"

Grandmommy reassures herself stepping toward the kitchen sink. "When Sherman gets here; if he wants to eat, he can, too," she again openly states while attempting to make dish water.

Khoi's already dressed for church.

I'm dressed, too, knowing in the back of my mind Aunt Gayla's going to show up any minute now. "I am not riding to church with Auntie Gayla!" I desperately tell Khoi.

"Well, you have to, Rhyah, because Grandmommy is still cleaning the kitchen.

Plus, she'll probably stay here with mama until we get back," he quickly lets me know wearing a phony grin.

. . . And just like clockwork, Uncle Sherman blows his horn for my brother to come on out. With his usual response, Khoi bursts through the screen door and down the sidewalk. The screen door bounces back just in time to swipe his left heel.

"Make sure you have your money for church, Khoi." Mama raises her voice to remind him.

She slowly moves toward the screen door expecting a confirmation.

Khoi, of course, knowing how mama is, slows down to slap against the side of his pants.

'Ka-ching, ka-ching' is heard. "They're both right here!" he yells back, after hitting the pocket where his two quarters lay.

. . . And sure enough, as predicted by Khoi, Auntie Gayla soon arrives to eat and then take me to church, too.

"Rhyah lets go. I'm through eating now. Khoi is already gone with your Uncle Sherman. Grandmommy is going to stay here with Vanessa," she exclaims at no surprise to me.

Before we leave, mama makes sure to straighten my hair bow. "Bows always make the package prettier," she smiles while giving a light pat on my shoulder. She probably couldn't gather the strength for a full hug.

"Khoi always ends up with the better deal!" I realize opening up Aunt Gayla's car door.

On the way to church, I instinctively sit with my legs perfectly crossed.

"Young ladies are to be seen and not heard," Aunt Gayla would lash-out if she even thought I was not being lady-like.

"Keep your chin up," Is what she likes to say when I'm quoting bible verses to her.

"Smile, but don't show all of your teeth."

"Always pronounce your words clearly."

"Don't use slang or it'll make you appear uneducated."

I don't know about Khoi, but sometimes I feel like a trapped rat when I'm alone with her.

Oh! And her song and dance routine about always making eye contact is another story.

I knew the worst was yet to come this morning as she began to ask, "What have your grades been like?"

"I dunno. *Good*, I guess," I reply warily knowing there's going to be a follow-up to *any* answer I provide.

"*WELL.*

You mean—*WELL*, Rhyah!"

"Huh, I don't understand?

What are you talking about, Auntie Gayla?" I ask, confused about what she's trying to correct me on this time.

"When a person is stating a positive condition pertaining to something or someone, the reply should always be '*well*' and not '*good*'".

"Ok, *well*, I guess." I repeat imitating her in my mind.

"Rhyah, a good education is very important. One day, you are going to be a doctor, a lawyer, or maybe a great orator."

With a puzzling look, "What's an orator?" I inquire.

"An orator is a person who is able to speak to a very large audience and keep their attention all at the same time," she proudly tells me.

Well, what I figure is that she's the one who should have been a 'great orator' since she talks so much while trying to maintain everyone's attention—*all at the same time, too!*

CHAPTER 5

The Crystal Angel

No sooner than reaching O'Peniel's foyer, Khoi leaps from behind one of the church's double doors, teasing me about having to ride to church with Aunt Gayla this morning.

"I bet you couldn't even move, huh?" he mentions with a smirk about his face. "I bet you had to use complete sentences, too, huh?" He adds.

"The other boys and I have been playing since we got here," Khoi again sneers wiping off his pants. After that, he sprints back toward the church in order to return to the sanctuary; only to take his seat near Uncle Sherman.

I hear the choir singing off key—as always. Hopefully, this is their last song of the service. I intentionally pause in the foyer before making my way into the sanctuary; stalling for time just in case it's not their final song. In my opinion, all choir members should at least be required to know how to sing before participating in one.

Basically, the only two things in this foyer are a gold tray, which holds those church fans over there and a crystal angel that hangs on a hook right below the entryway into our sanctuary. The tray must be made of fake gold because its handle and sides are peeling; leaving a silvery-dull color underneath. Members of O'Peniel never forget to pick up a fan out of the tray before they enter our sanctuary. They'll grab one as quick as you can swat at a fly. At this particular time, the tray is just about empty because church has already begun.

Oh, Yes! And there is a third thing; a small brown table in which the fan tray sits on. I had forgotten about that table because it's so unbalanced until it has to rest against the wall in order to stand upright. It's like this because one of its legs is barely hanging on. I know because I inspected it one other Sunday morning. Instead of Rev. Reeves spending the church's money to have red dirt laid down, he should have had some of the old furniture replaced.

Other than that, there isn't anything else in here, except for the white paint on its walls.

Just to add, each time I pass through here, I always notice that crystal angel seems to have the ability to observe you no matter where you are in the sanctuary. *It'll look directly at you as if it is trying to tell you something.*

My family says that Papa Joseph hung the angel in the foyer in case someone had made their own guardian angel mad before coming to church. At least they'd still have one before they entered the sanctuary.

There's something *special* about this crystal angel, though. It's only about . . . umm . . . I'd say 3 to 4 inches long . . . and about 3 inches wide. No more than about 5 inches, or so, long, though. Yeah, that sounds about right. It's special because it *hangs up there at attention. Like a soldier about to go to war.* This is probably how the angels in Heaven appear, too; *always ready and waiting to serve God.*

It has wings that are evenly spread apart, but tucked away at both end-tips.

Its face and upper body are smooth, but shapely. The eyes look piercing enough to read into *the soul.* No halo around its head, unlike on the church fans. I thought all angels had halos, though. Maybe that is what makes this angel so extraordinary. Its lower portion has pleats carved into it. These pleats run long-ways similar to those of a bride's wedding dress. There does not appear to be any feet that I can tell of. Angels really do not need 'em, anyway. What purpose would they serve for an angel? It's not like they have to walk while trying to get around . . . That's what their wings are used for.

What I envision is that guardian angels fly around protecting us on Earth when they are not serving God in other ways or singing praises in Heaven.

The announcements are being read as I finally enter the sanctuary.

Aunt Gayla has already taken her seat. The church is full of waving fans.

Sis. Pearl, one of our ushers, waves her hand fan to get my attention; letting me know where Aunt Gayla is sitting. I'm so glad the choir has finished '*whining*' and is now seated.

Sis. Bradley, the organist, has already taken her seat near the choir stand.

Among reading other notices, the announcement clerk mentions that 'Children's Day' is to be held next month. A sign-up sheet for all children's duties is to be placed in the foyer next to the fan tray at the end of service.

The deacons rise in order to collect the initial offering of the day.

CHAPTER 6

The Pulpit I

As Rev. Reeves prepares to take to the pulpit, church members readjust their bodies and begin raising their fans. All around, these fans appear as straight as a deer's antlers. He leaves his study a few minutes early today.

"Uh, I wonder why?"

Probably to scope out the crowd for his intended victim, I'm sure.

Look at him with his scary self; sitting up there so impatient.

Waiting (and watching) while the deacons finish collecting all the offerings."

As my eyes scramble around the sanctuary, Aunt Jan's fan, especially, is positioned—as if to say she's ready for Rev. Reeves' sermon. She's sitting two pews up, just to the right of us. She holds her fan so close to her face that I can barely see her eyes. A Halloween mask with hair budding from both sides of it is what she looks like.

Aunt Jan is Grandmommy's youngest and smartest sister. We always have a lot of fun when she's around. She can hold a long conversation about any topic.

Hmm! Maybe, she was once a great orator.

When she and my Uncle Leon, her husband, get to talking, you want to call—"TIME-OUT!"

Each one of 'em will go to any length just to prove their point. Uncle Leon is a Dean at the junior college here in town.

Mama jokes that he and Aunt Jan are 'tit-for-tat.'

Aunt Jan recently commuted to a major university not too far from here to obtain her Master's Degree in Economic Policies. She did it just to prove to my Uncle Leon that he was not smarter than her. As a matter of fact, at her graduation ceremony, Aunt Jan shocked the crowd and my family when she grabbed the microphone and yelled, "Leon, this one is for you, babyyyy!"

I laughed, but most of my family covered up their faces with their ceremonial programs as if they were using hand fans at O'Peniel.

With a scattering mind, I remember that Aunt Jan used to be our church's bookkeeper. She and Rev. Reeves had a *falling-out* about the record keeping procedures. Aunt Jan wanted to continue keeping the books as she had done when my grandfather was preaching here. After Rev. Reeves came and he wanted it done his way. Eventually, Rev. Reeves won the battle. And he finally appointed someone else because Aunt Jan refused to change her ways.

The offering plate is currently passing from hand to hand on the row ahead of us.

Aunt Gayla gives me a one dollar bill to put in it. She took it out of her coin purse. A fancy looking, little purse that's colored brightly with pink and green—her sorority colors.

"Thank you, Auntie Gayla.

Mama forgot to give me my quarters."

"Sure sweetheart, that's o.k."

"Hmmm, she's not so bad", I state to myself thinking about how mama only gives Khoi and I a quarter for each offering.

The marquee' mentions that today's sermon will be 'Keeping Your House Clean.' With a topic like that, Rev. Reeves is sure to pounce on someone as he does on most other Sunday services.

I made sure that I used the bathroom before leaving home.

For one, Aunt Gayla is sorta like mama, you have to sit still in church. But, on top of that, one might miss some action when the drama scenes begin to unfold in here.

Rev. Reeves finally approaches the pulpit and ruffles through the pages of his ol', worn bible. His eyebrows rise to the top of his head. Wearing a frown, he looks through his bible intently. Intense enough that he's pinching the lower corners of each page.

He searches through it as if he'll be unable to begin today's sermon unless he finds what he's particularly looking for.

Yanking real hard to the right!

Then, only stopping long enough to lick a couple of finger tips!

Uh . . . Oh . . . now, that's a new move . . .

A *quiet panic* erupts in the pews.

Then, he snatches some of those same pages back to the left.

His search ceases with him pressing into the creased portion of the bible. He presses slow, but hard with his thumb.

He apparently finds a specific page and unexpectedly seems to relax a bit.

As a result, I notice that a few hand fans in several of the members' hands do, too.

Soon after that moment, he begins with, "The body is your temple.

You have to keep it clean and pure.

That, which reeks of *havoc* within or around you, must be *dispelled* of."

"Huh?

What?

What is *habbuck*, Auntie Gayla?"

"Is it some type of meat or something?" I begin questioning her and looking around to see if anyone near me might have some.

". . . And what kinds of *spells* is he talking about that's in here." I persist as I look around for mists in the air.

Expectedly, "Ssshhh," Aunt Gayla responds.

"Your spirit must be clean and of goodness; not of filth.

Garbage in causes garbage to come out," Rev. Reeves says with his bible pressed against his chest.

"Keep a clean house.

Clean it UP!

Clean UP your houses t-o-d-a-y!" He shouts into the congregation as if he's throwing a kiddie tantrum.

With his arms swinging wildly, Rev. Reeves takes his thick bible and hits it on the edge of the pulpit—so hard it flies up and onto the floor.

Pages are flying everywhere!

Some float around as if they were Khoi's paper airplanes.

One page gets caught-up in the wind of a box fan and flies off near the foyer. About 10 or so pages finally land on the floor while several others drift aimlessly throughout the pews.

A couple of pages land next to Sis. Bradley's right foot. Appearing frightened, "Ewwww!" is the sharp, shrieking sound she makes before quickly sliding her foot over as if those pages are hissing rattlesnakes.

Khoi and the group of boys near him begin to snicker.

Next to another loosely fallen page, Rev. Reeves' raggedy bible cover lay there on the floor split wide open.

O'Peniel's members remain calm, but nervy.

Calm—in a collected type of way.

Nervy—as for the way they're keeping strong grasps on their hand fans.

No one . . . not even any of the deacons, venture to pick up any of the scattered pages.

Rev. Reeves' words today are scattered, but striking.

His weird actions are, too!

Something like the way my brother cuts our grass if mama has not called the yardman in several weeks; complete, but incomplete, too, in a strange sorta way.

With my eyes flipping about, I keep seeing O'Peniel's members' fingers continuing to grip strongly onto their fans.

CHAPTER 7

The Pulpit II

Seeing the congregation's reactions this morning reminds me of a sermon he preached about three months ago. I'll never forget how strongly he preached that Sunday morning. The subject was "Keeping On The Straight and Narrow!"

Aunt Norice was his *trophy prize* that morning.

Aunt Lorice and Aunt Norice are twins. Grandmommy came first, then the twins and finally, Aunt Jan. Actually, Aunt Jan is not too much older than my mama.

Grandmommy is the only quiet one in the bunch. I hope to be just like her if I someday become a grandmother; always *'stepping out of self'* to be gentle and caring. By nature, she easily holds to her unyielding morals. Her principles concerning life always seem to be generated from the heart.

Grandmommy's twin sisters are twins for a reason; they are just alike.

You can tell they're twins mainly because they both wear long, silky wigs with curls that flow like waterfalls. They'll do anything to attract attention, in my opinion, especially my great Aunt Lorice. Aunt Lorice isn't married, but Aunt Norice is. Uncle Benny, her husband, doesn't come around much.

Unlike Uncle Leon (my Aunt Jan's husband), Uncle Benny (my Aunt Norice's husband), does not show his face too much. Nor, does Uncle Benny participate in our family's get-togethers. He just stays to himself most of the time never attending anything, for that matter.

Besides leaving the house to go crabbing or fishing, he mainly sits at home smoking cigars and watching the cable news networks repeat the headlines of the day.

Grandmommy believes that being a long-haul truck driver for so many years made him generally prefer to be in his own company.

I guess he's just still used to being alone primarily because of those long periods of time on the road. For that reason and in many ways, it's like my Aunt Norice isn't married, either.

Anyhow, I still cannot figure out why Rev. Reeves made an example out of Aunt Norice on that given Sunday, other than that she gives wild card parties sometimes.

Her parties seem to be better than the ones mama throws during Mardi Gras season. Uncle Benny sits in their bedroom not participating in these parties. Some of O'Peniel's members will come to Aunt Norice's gatherings. They'll laugh, drink beer, smoke cigarettes and discuss anyone's business that was not present that night.

An account I've overheard Aunt Gayla tell so many times is when Bro. Carrington, O'Peniel's head deacon, was caught at one of her parties feeling on mama's knee under a card table. Story had it that he tried to lie and say that he was giving mama a cue for the next play. Bro. Carrington was not even Mama's card partner that night. His own wife, Mrs. Carrington, was.

CHAPTER 8

The Pulpit III

Rev. Reeves is still standing up there shouting, but doesn't seem to be delivering his messages toward any one in particular this morning. He has not even picked up his bible or its loose pages from the floor.

"Stop moving around! And definitely stop that daydreaming you seem to do all the time! Have respect! Rev. Reeves is still preaching, Rhyah," Aunt Gayla sternly tells me.

Then, she whispers, "Be still and I'll take you to Harry's Donut Shoppe after church.

My only reply is a smile, because I know that I'll now have one over on Khoi.

Aunt Gayla, and of course, Grandmommy seem to give Khoi and I *waaaay* more treats than mama does. Aunt Gayla just asks too many questions about dumb stuff, but Grandmommy will give us anything without any questions being asked.

I know my mind is dancing all over the place, but it's still not clear who Rev. Reeves will choose as his 'prize' for today, but earlier I did see him slap his bible against his own chest a couple times during a screaming episode.

And just a minute ago, he did slip and say the word '*me*' *in regard to himself* instead of referring to '*the congregation*' *as a whole* as he preached about choosing to walk in the light.

He tried to cough-over 'his mistakes' in order to erase them, but I clearly heard what initially came out.

I've noticed that he has not been doing his usual staring (scouting in search of a victim) at anyone in particular today. I've been waiting for it, but those cold eyes of his have not become attached to anyone seated out here yet.

Maybe he had planned all along to chisel his own self this morning.

"Nope!

No way!"

He tries to act like he's too perfect.

Always walking around as if he's without fault and spying on people.

One of the deacons, maybe?

One of those ol' ladies in the choir or even an usher, possibly?

Could it be one of 'em? I imagine, not having a clue as to who today's victim may be.

Nah!

He surely wouldn't turn to where any of 'em are sitting and stare 'em down.

After all, deacons are considered up-standing officials in the church.

A visitor, perhaps . . . No, it couldn't be one of 'em, either. That would only give a bad first impression of our church.

Plus, choosing to stare at a visitor would be waaaay too noticeable—

Well . . .

Or, then again, what would he care?

Huh! On the flip side, anything's possible with Rev. Reeves.

"*'I'*" Rev. Reeves jolts from his throat. And then quickly clears his throat to instead say "'***the church***' must remain focused in God's divine fortitude."

"Oh! Yes!" he wails while balling up a tight fist. "This is the only way to keep *my temple*, uh, uh, ***our temples*** clean. A sheep knows its shepherd's voice, O' dear Lord. By means of Your divine grace, please allow *me,* uh, uh, ***us*** to never again go astray!

Let *me*, I mean, **let us** always continue to see and hear your wisdom actively working within us. Oh Lord, pleaseeeee help *me*, . . . *us* . . . *us* . . . *us* . . . **help us** to not walk by sight, but by enormous faith as Your word commands. Throw away that in *me* . . . **I mean in all of your children** that houses filth and restore *my soul* . . . **our** . . . **our** . . . **restore our souls** with new ones", he says after clearing his throat again.

Rev. Reeves becomes silent.

He appears to be replaying his own words in his mind as his eyes swing up toward Heaven.

He releases his balled up fist to reach for his handkerchief that's crouched in a front pocket.

He takes one deep breath—a very slow one to be exact.

And then another even longer one after wiping the sweat from his face and neck.

He allows his face to rest in the handkerchief for a second or two.

"Is he praying? It sure seems so." I both question *and* provide an answer for myself.

Following an additional outburst, Rev. Reeves slightly lifts an arm.

There is no escape from the clear ring of sweat that's plainly showing under his arm.

"Why is he doing that?" I ask loudly pushing forward in my seat.

Aunt Gayla, also caught -off-guard by his actions, doesn't answer me.

Rev. Reeves shoves the handkerchief back in his shirt's front pocket.

Afterwards, he slowly removes his eyeglasses from his face.

He pauses again. But, only long enough to wipe any remaining moisture from the lenses.

"What is he doing?" I ask again; this time while lifting my body and stretching my neck forward.

Aunt Gayla, not knowing what to say, continues to ignore my requests—like mama often does.

Then, Rev. Reeves once more extends his arm upward. But this time, as far as it can go.

He closes his eyes, postponing further actions for a quick moment.

So do all the waving church fans.

He lays his other arm across his chest making a half 'X' and slightly rares backward.

The church is silent . . . and so is he.

As my eyes chase around the pews, the only apparent activity is some more of Rev. Reeves' sweat dripping off his face.

That, along with the hum of the box fans . . . and Bro. Campbell quietly snoring.

Has Rev. Reeves, himself, just **'come face to face with God'**? I think to myself.

Sis. Bradley begins to chime-in on her organ.

Rev. Reeves stands there for another moment.

Heavier drops of sweat continue to plop down.

He opens his eyes without parting his lips.

For some reason, it seems as though he'd glanced at the foyer before loosening his rigid stance to take his seat. "I don't know why he looked that way." But, from where he was standing, the only thing he could have noticed was *O'Peniel's crystal angel hanging on its hook.*

Even though today's sermon has ended, beads of sweat are still rolling down his face; down so far, at this point, they reach his chest.

"Hand me my purse, please. It's by your leg, Rhyah," Aunt Gayla requests just to purposely distract me.

At the moment, the deacons have begun collecting today's final offering.

Sis. Bradley uses one hand to play her organ and the other to fan Rev. Reeves.

His worn and torn bible still lay on the floor.

Aunt Gayla's shuffling through her coin purse once more to give me another dollar bill for the final offering.

"Rhyah, here's another dollar for the plate."

"Here."

With my mind still wandering, she finally hunches me and says, "This money is for the second offering. Also, we're leaving right after we've put our money in."

"Yes, ma'am." I answer back accepting the crisp bill.

The collection plate reaches me first. I drop my dollar in. Then, I pass it to Aunt Gayla, who in turn, gracefully places a small, sealed envelope inside. Her envelope was perfectly sealed and neatly written upon. Its letters didn't go below the lines nor were her numbers messy. How can someone always be so neat I wonder inside? "One day, you'll be tithing, too." She leans over to mention. She even took the time to elegantly pass the collection plate on down the pew.

Minutes later, we get up to leave my brother behind with my Uncle Sherman and his four step kids. Before departing the foyer, Aunt Gayla signs my brother and I up to participate in the annual 'Children's Day.' She finally signals goodbye to Khoi and my Uncle Sherman and places her church fan back into its tray.

CHAPTER 9

Proof of a Wedding

"Aunt Gayla, don't forget to stop for my donuts." I remind her leaving O'Peniel's parking lot.

We pass Uncle Sherman's big truck prior to kicking up clouds of red dust.

"Aunt Gayla!

Look.

Uncle Sherman still has the horse trailer attached to his truck from yesterday."

"He needs a big truck," she begins with a smile, "At least to provide room for his long legs and space for wearing those cowboy hats, Rhyah." "Yea", I reply in my mind, "He owns about 20 of 'em."

Uncle Sherman does not have any children of his own.

He married Aunt Margie over 2 years ago downtown in front of a judge.

No one knew they were going to get married, either, on that spring day.

Not even my grandmommy! The next thing we all knew was that they had gotten married inside the gazebo that's stationed in front of the parish courthouse.

The proof: wedding pictures he carried around in his wallet and their gold, wedding bands. "No diamonds?" I remember Aunt Norice having asked him.

It is a nice gazebo, I recall in thinking back. As a matter of fact, in front of the gazebo is where our Black History Parade always begins and ends.

The parade will kick off there before winding around our town square and through some more city blocks. Afterwards, it ends right back up at that gazebo with beads being thrown.

Khoi and I used to play inside of the gazebo when mama was in town paying bills.

We'd jump off its huge, concrete steps and then race to the courthouse.

White, with honey suckle vines weaving in and out of it, is what I remember mostly about the gazebo. There were always fresh flowers planted around it, too. We'd pick those flowers and give 'em to mama as a surprise.

But, why would anyone want to get married outside, anyway, with all those bugs flying around?

Especially, with these swamps and bayous bringing about mosquitoes. Flies, too.

Or, what if it had begun to rain that day?" I say silently riding pass these tall pines trees.

Aunt Margie is Kristy, Morgan, Paul, Jr. and Marcus' mother. The Sunday after she and my uncle married, Rev. Reeves' sermon topic was 'Harvesting a Good Crop'. I remember my Uncle Sherman holding his fan's thin, wooden, handle so tight, it cracked. After church, he stood by his truck picking tiny splinters out of his thumb.

I'll never forget parts of that sermon because that was *some* day, for sure.

Yes, indeed, it was!

I remember Rev. Reeves' remarks oh, so well because he moved *beyond* the pulpit that day in clear view of Aunt Margie and my Uncle Sherman to deliver his words.

"You reap what you sow! Seeds grow best in fertile soil, not from an uncultivated land. An untamed crop is a crop that will never bring about a proper harvest," He frankly kept declaring while aiming his bible toward 'em.

"A union from Heaven must be equally yoked!" he kept inserting through out the sermon.

He must have banged that bible against that pulpit fifty times or more that morning.

To me, it was obvious that our pastor didn't agree on 'em having gotten married.

Aunt Margie, herself, must have realized it, too.

I know.

Because she has not been back to O'Peniel since that day.

Khoi not only enjoys being with Uncle Sherman, but with his step kids, too.

I don't, however! Kristy and Morgan poke fun at me.

They say my hair bows are longer than my hair. Even though mama makes sure my hair is taken care of, it still doesn't seem to grow as fast as theirs.

Or, stand out like theirs always does, either. Their hair is thicker looking than mine.

Some Sundays, they get to wear their long hair down like grownups; full of curls or styled like the older girls wear their hair; full-looking with a lot of body.

Despite my numerous requests to do the same, mama won't dare let me.

"You have plenty of time to do things like that, Rhyah Ann," she always concludes.

I used to wear bangs. They made fun of those, as well, saying I looked liked like a toy baby doll with 'em hanging off my forehead.

They inspect me as if they are on a mission; always looking me up and down and then making nasty remarks afterwards.

"What for?" I often wonder as we near the donut shoppe.

I surely don't know. We are all along the same age. I admit, I am a little jealous of their hair, but I don't know what their problems are.

"What could be so different between 'em and me?"

Mama says to just ignore the both of 'em because they probably want to be my friend, but they just do not know how to go about doing it.

Marcus and Paul, Jr. call me *'church-cross'* when adults aren't around.

Now, that really picks at my nerves! In church, if no one's looking, they'll put their arms straight-out like a small letter 'T' and they won't move 'em for a long period of time. Ugh!

They make me so sick! They do it because when I'm seated by mama, I have to forever sit straight-up.

Still and stiff; just like a cardboard cross. No, like two boards nailed at the center.

Straight-up. Sorta like the way I am sitting right now in Aunt Gayla's car.

To say the least, I sure wouldn't want to get her all riled up again about how a young lady is supposed to act.

I have told mama that Marcus and Paul, Jr. do this to me. And I've even hinted to her that I hope Rev. Reeves catches 'em one day and screams at 'em during one of his sermon of fits . . . and I cannot wait for that day, either!

Mama, on the other hand, had a simpler reply for me.

"Be careful what you wish for, Rhyah Ann," she advised.

CHAPTER 10

The Donut Shoppe

We reach Harry's Donut Shoppe. It's located in the south end of town—inside a parking lot that's full of pot holes. Aunt Gayla dodges every one of 'em and whips into a corner parking spot beating an ol' man to it.

Out of aggravation, the man releases his hands from his steering wheel. He throws 'em up as if Auntie Gayla meant to purposely cut-off his ol', grey pick-up truck. She doesn't even realize what she's done.

But, I did.

I notice everything.

Always. All of the time.

I also notice he's missing his rear bumper as he turns his truck around to back up and park elsewhere.

"BELEVE?"

"Huh?" I wonder.

The word 'BELEVE' is on his personalized license plate.

It hangs in the rear window of his ol' truck.

"B—E—L—E—V—E?" I spell-out letter for letter in my mind.

"That doesn't look right!" I assume again looking back toward the ol' man's truck.

I question the word's proper spelling; unsure why this would appear on a person's license plate, anyway.

"Wait a minute!" I begin to speculate unlatching my seatbelt.

"Something seems different" . . . I continuing wondering looking in his direction once more.

I become aware that there's a missing letter in that word.

'I.'

"The letter 'I' is what's missing," I conclude wishing my dictionary weren't at home, but with me.

Hmmm, I see why my family is always speaking about the importance of a good education. This person can't even spell!

'Believe'! Believe what?

Is this man *seeking attention* by using a misspelled word?

Or, is he trying to make a *statement* by using a misspelled word?

I attempt to ask Aunt Gayla what the man is possibly trying to prove, but she cuts me short me to graciously say, "You may have up to 3 donuts if you wish."

Aunt Gayla makes this statement as a whiff of fresh baked breads seeps into her sunroof. A burst of cinnamon flows into the car once we open our car doors.

She gets out very ladylike and dignified; holding her dress tail, but maintaining good—posture, too; sorta kinda in a way as to not lose her balance.

Aunt Gayla always wears high heels to church and to work.

She's strutting up the sidewalk in 'em right now . . . all prim and proper like.

Her heels always seem to match her dresses perfectly. Even the jewelry she selects always seems just right for any of her outfits.

Nearing the front door, "Let's not be too long in here," Aunt Gayla forcibly mentions.

A large wall of glass separates two men who knead and twist dough as if their hands are bread machines. Covered in white flour, their hands steadily throw big globs of dough around. There seems to be enough flour on the floor and on their shoes, altogether, to make another entire batch of dough.

In the front and on the other side of the glass wall stands a woman behind a counter.

Oh yea. This reminds me. I remember when Khoi and I were smaller, the counter ladies would issue glazed scrap pieces made from leftover dough to all kids who came in.

"It is not too crowded. I guess we came at a good time. Oh look! The sign is blinking," Aunt Gayla says as she opens up their noisy door for me. There's a rusty bell propped up on the door. It rings when the door is opened, but they can take it down because the door alone makes plenty of noise. Besides, that bell is barely hanging to the yarn it's tied to.

Aunt Gayla starts looking at a worker shuffle an arm full of dough toward a flour-covered table. He gets my attention, too, when he flops it down—scattering even more flour onto the floor. He then quickly chops the dough into sections before stretching and pulling on it. "Rhyah," Aunt Gayla informs me, "This place has been here since your mama, Sherman, and I were little kids." Afterwards, Aunt Gayla takes another look up at the blinking sign.

Oh! And another thing: when Khoi and I were younger, we did come here more often. Daddy would bring us when we were bored. Mama would bring us when she was out running errands. Now it seems like we only come several times a year. From the high way, we'd see that the sign blinking and beg for mama or daddy to stop. I really couldn't read what the letters said back then, but, I sure knew seeing these gold and red colors twinkling back and forth meant hot donuts.

Khoi and I would stand against the glass wall watching the men make donuts while the icing drooled down our hands and face. Khoi used to draw figures on the glass wall with his extra icing. Oh, yea. Grandmommy used to bring us here a lot, too. But, when she'd bring us, she never complained about the messes we'd make in here, but mama and sometimes daddy would get upset.

The 'Hot Donuts Now' sign blinks when donuts are freshly made. It's kind of like the marker for this place.

A trademark.

Yes! Now that is a better choice of word.

A trademark.

The blinking sign is this place's trademark just like the fans are O'Peniel's trademark. The word 'Hot' blinks in gold and 'Donuts Now' follows up in red. Seeing this sign makes my mouth water because the donuts will still be warm with melting icing.

The woman behind the counter is lucky she gets to work around sweets all day.

I would love to have a job like this when I begin working. I could always lick bowls of icing; then, eat sugary beignets or hot donuts with lots of candy sprinkles all day if I wanted to. I wouldn't want to wear that hospital-looking cap on my head that she's wearing, though.

"Rhyah, stop looking around and stop that day dreaming you always do. Choose something—PLEASE!" she reminds me in a proper, but stern way.

"Oh! I would like two chocolate covered donuts and one cinnamon-sugar covered donut." I turn back around to look through the glass; taking another glance at the men making donuts.

"Please!" Aunt Gayla redirects.

"Oh! I'm sorry. Please, ma'am." I rightfully reply.

The woman behind the counter nods and smiles. Then, reaches under the counter for a wax-coated bag and two pastry tissues. Instead of getting my donuts off the tall, horizontal, shelves behind her, she goes around to the other side of the glass wall.

Over there, the donuts are only minutes old.

Hot! . . . and . . . Fresh!—because that's the best time to eat 'em!

She tries to pick up two chocolate covered donuts at one same time.

But, can't.

They're too soft and fluffy.

So soft and so fluffy they immediately go limp on her which makes her have to get them one by one . . .

Then, the woman re-dips the two donuts (one at a time) into a bowl of melted chocolate; giving me extra icing.

She recoats my cinnamon-sugar donut in the same way.

"Just the way I like 'em, too!" I state smiling inside.

"That'll be one dollar and 14 cents," the lady says wiping away extra chocolate from her hands.

My Aunt Gayla gives her exactly one dollar and fourteen cents out of her two-toned coin purse.

She hands the lady one of her crisp dollar bills, first.

Then, two nickels.

And lastly, four pennies. Four shiny and new-looking pennies, at that.

Aunt Gayla cautiously gives the woman her money by counting the amount of each coin out-loud as she places it in the center of her hand.

I guess she's picky about her money, too.

"Thank you."

"You're welcome." the Aunt Gayla replies.

"Rhyah, let's go." Auntie Gayla says after motioning for the receipt.

Aunt Gayla doesn't get anything for herself; only some napkins and I'm pretty sure that those are for me.

A pile of napkins lay next to the cash register. Instead of only taking several, Aunt Gayla grabs a heap of 'em along with her receipt.

Reason for the large amount of napkins—in my Auntie Gayla's mind—always be prepared for emergencies. Either that reason or she knew mama would have a *fit on top of fits* if I got my church dress dirty.

On the way out, our town's weekly, community newspaper catches hold of her eyes. These free newspapers are displayed next to the door on a rack. Aunt Gayla comes to a quick decision that I should eat my donuts right here instead of on the way home.

Current events about local schools and articles about area churches appear in it. Every time Grandmommy has a garage sale, she puts a notice about it in there.

But, for the most part, the newspaper's space is primarily taken up on grocery store advertisements for that week or other boring stuff.

In a rush-effort, Aunt Gayla has grabbed a copy and has headed toward a booth next to the door.

I follow her to see what's so interesting about this week's circulation.

Instead of taking the booth's seat across from her, I choose to sit right next to her.

I can't help but to peak at what the caption says that's also grabbing her attention.

We focus on a headlined article entitled "Black Women and Their Awesome Achievements." Next to the article, there are about four professional-looking women from New Orleans pictured in hard hats.

Leaning-in closer, chocolate icing begins to drip off my donut and down her left arm, then onto the table.

Annoyed by this, "Go and get some more napkins and have the lady to wet them for you, too, please!" she speaks in a frustrated, but polite manner. Having witnessed the whole incident and having overheard what Aunt Gayla's already requested of me, the woman behind the counter has already begun to adhere to my aunt's requests.

I hand Aunt Gayla the moist napkins. She begins to wipe her arm and clean up the small mess on the table. I, on the other hand, walk toward the glass wall endlessly amazed by the crafty way donuts are made.

These workers aren't even distracted by me. Nor, are they by the ol' man Aunt Gayla made mad earlier. He came in and took a corner booth near this glass wall some time ago.

All stretched out.

Relaxed . . . and sitting alone.

Seeming to not have a care in the world; only looking to take it easy. He did not get any donuts. Just a small cup of steaming, black coffee that he's been stirring since he sat down; slowly adding-in milk as if to get its color just right.

A customer leaving the Donut Shoppe breaks Aunt Gayla's concentration of reading the article. The screech of the door closing causes her to glimpse at her watch and then double-check its time against the clock in the Donut Shoppe.

"OH! M-y g-o-o-d-n-e-s-s!" she groans.

Rapidly, she gathers her purse along with the newspaper article that's been neatly torn out by now.

She slants her head upward to look my way. Before she could call my name, I begin to make a stride toward her, tripping over the ol' man's leathery boots. I did not see 'em. They must of blended-in with the floor.

I begin to stumble.

My waxy bag slips out of my hand.

In the act of bracing myself, the booth across from him helps to break my fall.

I regain my balance only to get a better look at the ol' man.

His clothes and boots seem as though he's been working since sun up in a sugar cane field somewhere.

His red eyes even show signs of hard work. The short, grey waves on both sides of his balding head are slicked back. So grey and so glossy; they remind me of thin shavings after a silver crayon has been sharpened.

"I'm sorry! It was an accident." I quickly roll out.

"Please excuse her, sir." Aunt Gayla says once she's rushed over to assist me.

"Are you o.k., Rhyah?"

"Yes, ma'am."

She, then, begins to brush my dress tail back down with her hands.

"Are you sure you're o.k., sweetheart?" The woman at the cash register asks stretching her body over the counter. Without any delay, Aunt Gayla replies, "Yes" while I shake my head up and down.

The man sluggishly bends down to recover my ripped bag from the floor.

My bag now has cinnamon-sugar mixed-in with the melted chocolate . . . and maybe a little dirt, too.

He slowly puts my torn bag onto the booth's table opposite him.

Definitely unhurried is how he moved.

A pace at which he does not have anything else to do for the rest of the day.

"Slow down, young lady. You are in such a rush just like she was earlier," he says, pointing a partially curved index finger at Auntie Gayla.

The aging man speaks slower than he moves. His words trickle from his mouth one by one with long pauses in between.

Presently, Aunt Gayla has a definite look of confusion on her face. She opens her mouth as if to speak, but, instead remains quiet. The wrinkles on his face and hands come across as warm, crimples of melted caramel after apples have been dipped in it.

The man gently sits back into his seat. His arched spine causes his body to somewhat lean a bit over the table. Sorta like the shape of his pointed finger. Aunt Gayla begins to plow through her purse.

"Now what did I do with my . . ." She starts out to say, but is unable to continue speaking because the ol' man has slowly slid his withered hand across the table to touch hers.

Shocked, she is unable to budge or get out another word; no more than to look at the man as strange as his actions seem.

Suddenly, he unexpectedly tells her to "slow down!" but in a hushed voice this time.

Only then does she cautiously reach to grasp my arm. By her own actions, I can tell Auntie Gayla is not used to people telling her what to do, especially an unfamiliar person.

And he has the nerve to touch her while saying it, too!

His lower arms are tanned with that caramel color, but the top parts of 'em have a lighter, more creamier color. About the same cream-like color as his coffee now that he's added all of that milk to it. What I assume is that his arms are probably like this from working out in the sun and simply wearing short sleeved shirts. The ol' man notices Aunt Gayla becoming uneasy. So, he removes his hand from atop hers, but not with any apparent speed. She, in turn, seems to lower her guard a little, too.

Slow.

Everything about this man seems to be slow with some sense of control concerning his every move.

He must live a slow motion lifestyle.

"How boring", I think to myself.

All of a sudden, Aunt Gayla resumes fumbling through her purse.

She looks around for her keys.

"My keys", she lowly announces.

Her eyes sweep the floor.

She looks over her shoulder and afterwards—up toward the counter.

Panic sets in. I can tell because she's patting her foot with one hand on her hip.

"Now! Where! Are! My! Keys?" she worriedly phrases as she tosses up both hands.

Not realizing in her rush, she's left 'em back on the booth's long chair we'd been sitting in.

After spotting her keys, I go to retrieve 'em myself. Then, to stand next to the door.

Seeing me gather 'em, "Oh, there they are," she exclaims in relief.

Afterwards, she starts toward the door, as well.

Never losing eye contact, the ol' man's red eyes connect with our every move.

Prior to me pushing open the squeaky door, he stops stirring his coffee to give additional words of warning.

"Take your time," he unhurriedly advises with his eyes fixed on Aunt Gayla.

"Then, you will hear God's plan. I saw you looking at your watch earlier; in such frenzy, then, you almost forgot your keys . . . moving so fast, you aren't even aware of your own surroundings."

"Slow down and listen!" he begins with a little more emotion in his voice. "Slow down!"

The woman behind the counter comes and stands in front of the cash register.

She obviously wants to hear what mellow words the ol' man has to say.

Not wanting to appear as if she's snooping, the woman did step aside and remove a full pot of coffee from its warmer. Expecting the man to carry on, little by little, the woman inches closer toward the section he's in, but never quite reaching his booth. She was just being nosey and not wanting to make it so obvious.

The ol' man gradually lowers his head with the intent to look at me.

I take Aunt Gayla's hand as his red eyes meet up with mine.

"Don't you, either, be in such a hurry, young lady, or you might miss out on a blessing. Seek His face and you will never miss a step."

The ol' man raises his head again. But, this time it's to continue speaking his very last words to Aunt Gayla. "Seek His face and not your own understanding and you will *always be on time.*"

With her purse clutched under one arm, Aunt Gayla grips the newspaper article with the opposite hand.

There's no response from her.

No facial expressions, either.

Stagnant is how I currently describe her mood.

She only stands here plainly gripping at what's all in her possession; her purse and the article.

Afterwards, she nudges me to keep on out the door.

Aunt Gayla does not look back.

But, I do.

I can't help it.

I see that the ol' man is stirring his coffee, but continuing to watch us as we get back into Auntie Gayla's car. His large veins seem to be bulging right through his wavy skin.

Aunt Gayla, cautious as ever, still has not parted her lips.

She doesn't even get back into her car in a graceful routine.

This time, she quickly plops into her seat, rescues her keys from me and starts the engine.

She gets in so quickly that she closes the car door onto her dress.

"Aunt Gayla, your dress . . ." and before I could finish telling her, she opens up her door and grabs the dress without mentioning a word.

I again fasten my seatbelt securely. It's a safety requirement, if you know what I mean, when she's behind the wheel. Plus, if I don't fasten it right away, I'll have to hear another lecture on how seatbelts save lives.

Peering over, I see that her seatbelt has not even been touched as we pull away.

Aunt Gayla has to swerve several times to miss the pot holes. I adjust the strap on my seatbelt in order to look back toward Harry's.

In doing so, I still see the ol' man staring at us and finally taking a sip of his coffee.

His face lingers in my mind as I wonder how he's perched there in his seat.

His hands huddled over that cup of coffee.

His arched back.

His red eyes.

Unusual enough, he, too, displayed a facial expression that is indescribable—even for me.

Why? . . . Because with any sorta word, I can always describe any type of situation.

CHAPTER 11

The Ride Home

Trying to piece together what just happened; my mind begins to wander.

. . . And you know that this will clearly lead to questions.

"Aunt Gayla, what did that man mean when he said that I might miss a blessing if I don't slow down?"

"Rhyah, he was just making a *statement*, that's all.

Nothing to worry about," she declares with reassurance.

"'A *statement*?

A *statement* for what? . . . for what, Aunt Gayla?" I continue to question her about, but skip right on to say, "Yea, but, he didn't look like he, himself, had been to church at all today".

To the ol' man's defense, "Well, he may be Catholic. Some Catholics attend church on Saturdays", she quickly answers back.

". . . and what did he mean about seeking *His* face? Whose face?" I ask in order to get an understanding.

Aunt Gayla readjusts her rearview mirror. She's apparently collecting her own thoughts.

She also begins to reposition her sunroof. To get it positioned just right, she tilts it back and forth. At this point, she fastens her own seatbelt. Knowing that I am going to keep the questions coming, she informs me that, "The man was speaking about God. When a person is seeking guidance or needs help, people will often tell them to seek God's face," she states while drawing imaginary circles on her chest. "But more so, Rhyah, you should seek God in *everything*, not just when you're in trouble or need him to rescue you out of something. When bad times occur, there's always something good to come out of it that'll either teach you a lesson or that'll make you become a stronger person.

Ok.

But, not just in the bad times, you should seek Him in the good times, too. For He is always there with you in the *good times* and in the *bad!*"

I am trying to figure out her explanations, but am overly distracted by her never ending circles.

With my curiosity getting the best of me, "What's wrong with your heart?

Are you sick or something?"

Aunt Gayla, lost in thought, doesn't answer.

Still probing, I turn completely around to face her and finally inquire, "Why are you circling your heart in that way, Auntie Gayla?"

With a sophisticated chuckle, "Oh, no, Rhyah, I'm sorry. My mind was elsewhere.

I'm o.k.

I'm not sick at all."

She, then, places her hand back onto the steering wheel.

"It's just that I intended to explain that God reads your heart, too.

He searches it for your true intentions. A pair of lips can say anything. The tongue can be a sword. A person's mind can be poisoned, but one's exact intentions are written on the scrolls of their hearts."

I don't reply.

I'm thinking. And trying to make sense of it all.

Trying to visualize my heart turning into paper . . . and with words on it, too?

Instead, I sit still watching her pass other cars on the high way, but in the mean time, digesting all of this new information.

She turns on the radio to further distract my thoughts on the ol' man. Never leaving it on one particular station, but rather, switching back and forth through many stations till we reach my neighborhood.

"I hope to see mama up and about." I say, speaking over the radio while she also spins onto our street.

"Is mama going to be o.k, Auntie Gayla?"

"Yes, Rhyah," she replies with a look of confidence.

"God won't put anymore on your mama than she could handle. He never has and He never will with anyone."

'Powering-up', Aunt Gayla reaches to shift into another gear. Her shiny, sports car has a sound right now that means she's attempting to gain speed.

Our long street seems to turn into a some sorta stretch of raceway.

My left hand grips my seatbelt as she moves toward our house.

I clench my teeth.

My right hand is already tightly affixed against the door handle.

I brace to stabilize my body.

I await her next driving maneuver.

With my teeth clenched and eyes squoze shut; I remember why mama always tells my brother and I to wear our seat belts when riding with her.

What's about to happen next is truly a safety issue as far as I'm concerned.

Aunt Gayla makes a left tug at the steering wheel without changing gears.

Still traveling at the same rate of speed, our bodies sway right.

My head almost makes contact with the passenger side window.

The purple, gold, and green beads hanging from her rearview mirror swing out—so far wide, I feel 'em whisk by my left eye.

"Bloomp." We reach the edge of our driveway.

It's now that she decides to change to a lower gear.

The engine roars once more as Aunt Gayla scrams forward.

She doesn't hit the brake till we're about to stop.

"Skreeech!"

Our necks snap forward as the car comes to an immediate standstill!

After our short, motor-cross course, she yanks-up the emergency brake.

Slightly dizzy, I finally open my eyes to see her reaching into the back seat for her purse.

"I know your mama's probably waiting on us, so let's get out of the car," remarks Aunt Gayla seemingly unaffected by what I now judge as a 'dare-devil' stunt.

CHAPTER 12

No Picnic For Me

The family portrait of mama, my brother and I come to mind as we pass Khoi's football lying in the yard. Mama always hugs our portrait when we bring home good news. She'll cradle that picture frame and rock her body left to right as she listens to us. Today, my only good news is that Aunt Gayla has bought me donuts and Khoi, for once, has missed out.

"Mammmma!" I start off shouting running into the house. "We are back from churchhhh! Khoi is still with Uncle Shermannnn!"

The screen door bounces off my arm and slams in front of Aunt Gayla. She reopens it with a look of disgust toward me.

Neither mama or Grandmommy answer back. Just mere laughter in the background is the only response I get.

Inside the TV room, I see mama first. Her feet elevated atop two sofa pillows; appearing fine, just as Auntie Gayla had promised.

Grandmommy's seated on the sofa next to her. Every single blind and curtain has been pulled back in here. Yep! Grandmommy's presence is definitely around.

She enjoys a bright atmosphere.

"If the sun is out, let it shine and us receive it," she always says.

The TV is not on, just the stereo. Gospel music is playing and mama is looking much better. She and Grandmommy are giggling about something. Aunt Gayla places her purse on the coffee table and proceeds to join 'em.

Hi mama.

Hi grandmommy.

"What's that on your cheek, Rhyah?" Grandmommy asks standing up. She uses her thumb to wipe away the smudges.

"Chocolate probably," I answer, "We stopped by Harry's Donut Shoppe before coming home."

"Oh, how nice. I remember taking all of you there a many aday", Grandmommy replies with a smile.

I leave the TV room in order to keep my distance. I truly do not want to disrupt any ongoing conversations. Besides, Aunt Gayla (in her own particular way) would have said, "Rhyah, little girls don't need to be in a room where only grown folks are talking. Mama, though, would have put it plain and simple. She'd just come-on out with it by mentioning something like: "Rhyah Ann, why are you in here looking down our throats?" Grandmommy, not wanting to hurt my feelings, would otherwise keep sending me on little errands throughout the house. Grandmommy's errands are like: "Go and get me another cup of coffee; Go wipe your mama's windows sills for me in the living room; Have you straightened out your dresser drawers lately?"

Yes, indeed. This is the sorta stuff they'd all say if I'd have stayed in that TV room. So, you see, this is why I always try to keep my distance when I eavesdrop.

I begin to change out of my church dress and begin putting on my play-clothes.

In the distance, I hear them talking about the church picnic last summer from within my bedroom.

Still listening, more laughter erupts from within the TV room. That was a fun day and a lot of stories came of it, too.

I remember 'em all, too.

One specific story from that day is about my Aunt Jan and my Uncle Leon. They never showed up for the picnic that Saturday afternoon. They spent most of their day doing research, as usual, at our public library. They both spend time there and at the library on the junior college's campus whenever there's a dispute.

Before hand, my Uncle Benny had mentioned that the word 'picnic' meant something bad toward African-Americans. Because of this, he never attends any of 'em. Nope, if you call an outing a picnic, Uncle Leon will not go.

So my Aunt Jan convinced Uncle Leon to go and figure out where the word came from and what it *truly* meant.

Well, it all began when my Uncle Benny said that the word 'picnic' meant: to pick-a-nigger for lynching. He also told Uncle Leon that a long time ago; White people would gather outside by big trees and hang African-Americans—particularly the men.

After the lynching, the White people would then sit around eating and enjoying themselves while the victim hung from the tree. No one believed Uncle Benny, either. Mama said, "that something that sounds that strange couldn't be true." My dictionary pretty much stated that a picnic is an outing which includes a meal that's eaten outdoors. It did not mention anything about people; whether white or black. Or, about anyone being hung from any trees, for that matter.

So, anyway, my other great aunt and uncle got into a big debate over this *'one word'* on the day of the church picnic. We all had a great time anyway at O'Peniel's first annual picnic. DuPont's Smokehouse on Toulouse Street catered the event. All the ice-cold watermelon you could put down was set out on a single table near where the kids played. My brother and I ate mounds of potato salad. I drank so many red, cold drinks; my lips looked like Aunt Lorice's. We swam and played games for prizes. The adults received gift cards for bingo games they won that afternoon . . . and no one was hurt at our picnic, for sure.

I know.

I was there.

So, like mama, I don't know what Uncle Benny was talking about, either.

Uncle Leon and Aunt Jan never found out whether this was true or not and in the end missed out on attending the church's picnic.

CHAPTER 13

Thumps & Thuds = 'Ouch'

My play clothes are already on in-hopes that Khoi and I will be able to go outside this afternoon. "Ooops!" I forgot to ask mama if we could play outside while I was still in the TV room. Well, I'll start straightening up my bedroom right now so that she doesn't have any excuses later to say-NO!

They're still in there sitting on the sofa talking, but now in lower voices.

Not able to hear too clearly, I walk to the edge of my doorway placing my left ear nearest the TV room. The schoolbook I'm about to place into my backpack slips out of my hand. It slides down my right leg, aiming for my big toe. A corner of the book crashes into my toe and then flips over onto the floor causing a large, thud-like sound.

'THUMP'

"Rhyah, what was that?" mama interrupts their conversation to holler.

"Nothing!" I answer back.

Thinking that someone may be headed this way, I set in motion to turn back around; but, not before striking the left side of my head against the doorway.

'BOP!'

Another dull, but loud sound is made.

"Ouch!" I squeal in silence.

"Rhyah Ann, *WHAT* are you doing back there?"

"Uh, uh. . . . A . . . A book fell, mama," I reply, holding my head and trying to bend down to investigate my tender, big toe.

Limping and feeling a small knot form on the side of my head, I can barely make it to the bathroom Khoi and I share.

At last, I make it in here—with a continued effort to snoop, but trying to keep my balance (both at the same time). Our bathroom is situated near the TV room somewhat.

The guest bathroom, though, is always the neatest bathroom in the house because it's rarely ever used. It's even closer to them, but I would not dare have gone in there.

"What were my choices at that point?" I ask myself leveling my body up against the sink using my one and only 'good foot'.

It was either use this particular bathroom or try to make it to the kitchen for some ice.

Nah!

And risk mama, or even worse, Aunt Gayla asking a million questions about why I look so beat-up.

No-way, I'd rather suffer!

In here, I can at least run cold water over my toe and apply a wet towel to my head. Better still, I can safely listen-in on 'em from in here without being detected.

Their conversation takes another turn. Aunt Gayla informs 'em that she has signed me up to deliver the 'Children's Day' speech. She also tells 'em that she has signed up Khoi to lead the hour in prayer. Daddy always said that my brother would someday be a preacher or possibly a deacon.

"Hmmm . . . that's a joke!" I assume, letting the cold water pour over my toe.

A circus clown maybe. Or, even a stand-up comedian, but never a deacon or a preacher. But if anything, I think, he'll probably remain close to home since he tends to stick-up under my Uncle Sherman every chance he gets.

Grandmommy comments on what a big deal 'Children's Day' is at O'Peniel and how she thinks Aunt Gayla has signed my brother and I up for the best parts. For this annual occasion, children are scheduled to do everything, except preach, be ushers, or get the dinner plates ready after church service.

Other area churches visit, as well. Mount Calvary Baptist Church attends our program every year. Little Bethel Baptist Church, too. Little Bethel travels down here from somewhere near Baton Rouge.

Hobbling out of the bathroom, I hear Aunt Gayla informing 'em that Greater Mount Zion Baptist Church of Chateau Trinon will also be attending this year. The announcement clerk mentioned their acceptance of our church's invitation today.

When dinner is finally served to the adults, children take advantage of this time to play. Especially, since all children are fed first on 'Children's Day'.

Being back in my room, I envision myself giving my speech. My wet towel, a substitute for the speech's paper, is being held out before me.

I make believe my wall mirror is a movie camera.

My four-post bed is the make believe area in front of Rev. Reeves' pulpit.

Careful not to re-injure myself, I start practicing right away.

Everything is going to be perfect.

I know so.

Because thanks in part to Aunt Gayla's pushiness, I'm sure I'll get plenty of practice-time!

I sure hope this bump on my head goes down by then because I don't want anyone to misjudge this—'Black Cinderella' on that special day!

CHAPTER 14

Daylight Savings Time = Less Play Time

For the next couple of weeks, the weather continues to be easy-going.

Its early fall, but it still feels like the middle of summer.

The trees must feel it, too, because all their leaves remain a dark green. The only sign that fall has turned up is that it gets dark earlier in the evenings; cutting back on our playtime outside.

When we were younger, Khoi and I would complain about the time we'd lose by not being able to play longer during this time of year. Mama would have to go to the screen door numerous times to call us in. Confused about Daylight Savings Time, we'd whine about the time on the clocks.

"It's not even 5:30 yet, mama. Your news is still on," Khoi would protest.

In his defense, "Yea, we're usually still outside at this time." We haven't even heard the crickets begin to chirp yet," I'd tell her.

Not understanding why, she used to tell us every year that the moon and the sun had gotten their work schedules mixed up, so we needed to be inside so they could settle it. We believed her every time. And the next thing you knew, it would be spring time again and we'd have plenty of hours to play outside again.

Another thing, football season has begun; therefore Khoi's practices have, too. At the beginning of each season, mama always helps him get ready for his practices. There are a lot of pads with snaps he has to wear. Some of 'em makes him look as if he's wearing a diaper.

Right now, his team only practices two nights a week. Later, it'll probably move to four nights a week.

During football season, we get to travel to other towns to see his team play. Toward the end of last season, he played a game in St. James Parish.

Within this parish is a town known for its marshy grasslands. It's also where my other grand parents live. Mama has shown us their house from the high way, but we've never stopped. It's a small house that has a short, graveled driveway leading up to it.

Stubby and wide. That's what the driveway looked like to me.

Real stubby; similar to swollen thumb with only a nub for a fingernail.

Yea, short and sorta wide-like. But, only long and wide enough to fit one car in it.

CHAPTER 15

Hurry, please

Neither mama, nor Aunt Gayla are the organizers for the 'Children's Day' program that's less than a week away. But, they are running around town buying most of the items to be used for that day. They go out just about every evening this week buying items like: extra paper plates, napkins; stuff I haven't seen mama buy in a long time.

Aunt Gayla, as expected, makes sure that I know my speech 'down pat'!

I have to recite it to her every time she calls or happens to come by our house.

The eve of my *big day* has arrived! It's Saturday and I am so excited about my speech on tomorrow morning. Mama is, too, I think.

She's just finished frying catfish for lunch. We usually eat seafood on Friday's, but she took us to Pleasure Dome last night. That place is huge!

Its big, bubble ceiling makes you feel like you're in outer space.

Nothing but steel beams and a high, clear ceiling separated us from the stars and the moon yesterday evening.

There, we had 'Cajun-dogs'. These hot dogs buns with a spicy Andouille Sausage stuffed inside are always yummy. We all three used up a pocket full of tokens on arcade and racecar games and a lot of rides. I'm sure we rode everything out there twice or maybe even more.

Mama got dizzy and became nauseated on the 'Jerk 'm and Twist 'm Ride.

Luckily, this happened toward the end of the evening.

Khoi and I begged her to buy us a slice of pizza before leaving the indoor amusement center. Each slice was actually large enough for two people's enjoyment.

On the way home, we passed 'Tasti Freeze.'

"STOP, MAMA!

STOP!"

Khoi impatiently begged from the back seat.

Mama smashed on her brakes . . .

Threw on her left blinker . . .

Then, glided between two oncoming cars before pulling under the ice cream parlor's yellow awning.

We got there as a worker was changing the '*open*' sign to say '*closed.*'

"They've just closed, guys." Mama remarked with disappointment in her voice.

She noticed the saddened looks on our faces and said, "Hold on."

Mama, still sort of woozy, got out of the car last night holding the top of her stomach.

She left the engine running and her door wide open.

She approached the ice cream parlor's door.

"Bam! Bam!" she knocked.

She cupped her hands around her head to peak in using her headlights as her light.

She peered in at eye-level, and then squatted down to do it again.

After that, she beat on the door two more times. A young girl came up.

As I lowered my car window, I could hear mama telling the girl to please serve us.

She gave the girl some sob story in a low voice and kept pointing toward our car.

The young girl's annoyed facial expression turned to a look of sadness. A look that Khoi and I had on our faces just moments earlier. Needless to say, despite being closed, she agreed to let us in.

Mama was probably whispering in order for Khoi and I to not hear her as she gave the girl some sort of 'made-up tale.'

"Get my purse and close my door." mama yelled back toward the car.

She beckoned for us to hurry. "Don't forget to turn off the engine and my headlights," she finally shouted.

Still guarding the door, the young girl let us in before snapping shut every lock behind us.

Mama didn't bother to get anything for herself.

Her favorite ice cream is Chippy Chocolate Fudge. It's a milk-chocolaty ice cream with tiny, dark, fudge pieces mixed in it.

Right off, I knew what I wanted. I chose my favorite; a pint of Mountain Berry.

Khoi walked back and forth alongside a set of ice cream bins.

Then, he'd stroll beside another set of bins.

After that, he'd resume the same routine.

With her wallet already open, "You need to hurry up and order, Khoi!" mama insisted.

"I can't decide, mama."

He then proceeded to trail along two more bins gritting his teeth due to the agony of having to make a final decision. By then, his mouth and shirt were inseparable.

The girl was looking backward at the clock.

Its hands showed 10:18 pm.

She, too, awaiting his order, remained slumped over behind the counter.

"Hurry, son." Mama told him.

"Yeah. Time's-a-waist'n'," I whispered in agreeance.

"O.k., o.k., but I just can't make up my mind, ya'll."

The clock's reflection on an oversized, steel freezer now showed 10:22 pm.

After all that contemplating, he finally said, "Um, Um. O.k., I now know. I would like 1/3 Chunky Strawberry, 1/3 Gold Rush, and 1/3 Raspberry Mania."

Mama and I both sighed.

Mama sighed out of relief.

I sighed out of frustration.

The girl dropped both of her shoulders and also heaved a sigh. With that, she opened her mouth to release a smacking sound.

Afterwards, she rose up and slid back an ice cream bin's door rolling each eye in awkward directions. I guess, as to let my brother know she was agitated and frustrated, as well.

In the meantime, I had already begun tasting my ice cream. It was frosty and packed hard into the carton. Every mouthful seemed to freeze my tongue.

It was so stiffly frozen; I had to basically chew it. The three types of frozen berries were crunchin' in my mouth like hard candies.

Instead of gradually spooning out my ice cream from the carton, I basically had to use my spoon to cut it out. Funny, but what I really needed last night while eating my ice cream was a knife and fork. That's probably why the girl scooped our ice cream out using one of those flat-like scoops that resemble a small garden tool . . . instead of the more rounded type of scooper we have here at home.

Mama, still kinda woozy; began fanning herself while the girl retrieved Khoi's order.

The girl had almost finished preparing Khoi's pint when he decided that he yet wanted to add a fourth kind of ice cream—Cake and Cookie Passion.

"Could you squeeze some Cake and Cookie Passion in there for me, too, please? He relentlessly bolted.

Suddenly, mama jerked her head and body in his direction!

I felt a quick surge of wind by her sudden jolt.

"No!" Mama interrupted to shout, slamming her purse down on the counter.

Alarmed by mama's voice, the young girl jumped!

As a result of her high-pitched comeback, the girl jumped so hard, she smacked the top of her head against the bin's door.

"Uh, Uh!

No!

His previous order will be sufficient enough!" Mama demanded while shaking her head and continuing to fan herself.

Mama, the girl, and I all looked at Khoi who still did not appear to be satisfied with just having three kinds of ice cream.

Mama, all flustered at this point, rolled her eyes, quickly twitched her body both ways, and mumbled a few words under her breath at him.

Before the girl closed the lid on his carton, she plopped it down next to the cash register. Appearing slightly dazed, the girl took several steps back in order to zero-in on the bin that contained the Cake and Cookie Passion.

The clock hanging above her head read 10:33 pm.

After she had located it, she headed toward his fourth request.

On the way, she stopped to dip the scoop into a tray of cloudy water that had little berries (from my ice cream) floating to the top of it. Afterwards, she took the ice cream scoop and shook it hard. Real hard, too; along her left side; getting rid of any excess water. Having seen this, I knew then that that girl was gearing up for something.

Why?

Because with both hands, she stuck that scoop into that round barrel of ice cream and pulled up a huge chunk of the Cake and Cookie Passion.

Khoi's eyes were larger than silver dollars! His mouth, too, after his t-shirt fell from it!

The girl saw his contented expression and proceeded to dig out yet another chunk; the second scoop, larger than the first.

"Wow!" I thought to myself.

Since all the ice cream was obviously not going to fit into his first carton, she reached behind herself to get a whole new carton. As time conscious as I always am; and in between the girl moving around so much to fill Khoi's order, I had noticed that the clock had sprung to 10:39 pm.

Knowing he was gonna have way more ice cream than me, my brother was widely grinning. Not only did he bring home one carton full of ice cream last night; like magic, he instantly had two.

"Alllrightttt!

YES!

Thank you, ma'am!" Khoi told the young girl while mama was pulling out more money.

Massaging the top of her head, "That's o.k." the young girl said to mama.

"It's free . . . it's *alllll* free." She replied attempting to escort us to the door.

While leaving, I remember mama trying to thank the girl for our ice cream. Eventually, all I heard was a *'swish sound'*. It was the door closing quickly behind us.

"CLANK!" "CLANK!": were the sounds of her rapidly dead bolting both locks on the door. Needless to say, she wanted us out—QUICK!

I know we ended up angering that girl, but we walked out of there last night feeling satisfied and with more than enough ice cream, especially Khoi.

CHAPTER 16

Something Smells Good

The doorbell rings—breaking the focus of my ever-wandering mind.

Khoi and I dash to the front door.

"It's Grandmommy!" We boast looking through the screen door.

With a face full of joy, "Helloooo", Grandmommy drags out to greet us.

"Where's your mother?"

"In the kitchen," We again reply at the same time.

Side tracked by the smell coming from the kitchen, "I'm just dropping by. I had a few minutes to kill before going to participate in a Saturday afternoon Bridge Tournament." She mentions.

I still don't quite understand this type of card game. But, she must be good at it, though.

Her trophies highlight the fireplace's mantle inside her home.

When I was smaller, I thought Grandmommy and the people who played with her sat and built bridges out of cards. The group with the largest stack; the winner.

Grandmommy helps herself in the kitchen at preparing a catfish poor boy, first.

Afterwards, she returns to her car to surprise me with a new dress tucked away in a long zipper bag from Brideaux' Department Store. She brings the bag into the TV room and gracefully lays it across my lap. I'm overflowing with excitement because I've always assumed that most people would only shop there for very special occasions.

"Go ahead, take it out! It's for you to wear on Children's Day." Grandmommy anxiously tells me.

Hesitantly, I begin to unzip the long bag noticing a light fragrance coming from within it.

Swollen with joy, "Something smells good in here." I state.

"Oh yes, honey, that's the scent coming from the lovely coat-hanger.

Smells nice, doesn't it?" Grandmommy proudly informs me.

As I hold the bag in my lap, Khoi comes darting from out of nowhere.

He sticks his whole head in the bag to smell the scent, too.

"Stop!" I yell.

Still frowning, "You're going to mess my dress up!" I continue to shout.

In Grandmommy's usual hushed nature, "Step back a little, baby" she simply tells him.

"Look, mama! This padded coat-hanger has flowers printed on it, also.

I didn't know coat-hangers could be like this."

Mama grins at Grandmommy.

In the midst of my excitement, I also discover that she has bought me a matching hair bow to go with the dress.

Mama and I look over the dress inch by inch; feeling the fine material and admiring its design.

With a wink of the eye, "Khoi, go look in that other bag near my purse," Grandmommy hints. Khoi does not have to reach too far into the bag to realize that he has a brand new video game. Grandmommy and mama laugh as he runs into his room to play it; ripping off its entire clear, plastic wrapper with just one quick jerk.

My new dress is made of the kind of material that glamour models sachet around in on those home-shopping channels. It's black and trimmed in white with no buttons; only a zipper in the back.

"Oh look, there's also a jacket to match." Mama calls out.

The hair bow is made of the same smooth material as is my dress.

Grandmommy takes a pinch from her overstuffed poor boy and then reports to mama that, "this dress is part of Brideaux' newest fall-arrivals."

While grandmommy's still here, I run to my room to try my new dress on for her. As expected, it fit just fine on me.

CHAPTER 17

Eve of My Big Day

'Quiet as a bear's hideaway' is what my grandfather used to call calm Saturday evenings like today.

It's quiet in the house and I am bored to the bone.

I know it's late in the day now, but I just have to try this dress on again including its jacket. The new hair bow, too.

Too bad Grandmommy left before she could see me prancing and dancing around in it . . . and showing off in front of my mirror . . . and practicing my speech in it, too.

In between, I mentally picture how things on tomorrow morning will be.

In an instant, I become sidetracked by mama. Out of nowhere, she appears.

She sticks her head into my bedroom to disrupt my train of thought by saying,

"Remember what Gayla has written and how to pronounce the harder or longer words;

Remember how she wants you to stand;

Don't forget to pause after each and every sentence;

Make sure your hands are not swinging around;

Make sure you're looking straight ahead at the congregation;

. . . . and make sure . . ."

"Mamaaaa! I know! I know!" I say cutting her off at once!

"I told you earlier that I already knew what to DO and what to SAY!

Aunt Gayla has demonstrated a speaker's correct posture one million times for me.

She and I have rehearsed the speech two million times and you and I have gone over everything else three million times.

Hoping to ease her tension, "Mama! I—know—what—to—do!!" I openly advise.

"Allllrighty then." mama passively says as she pulls away from my bedroom door.

I'm left alone again for more quiet time to continue imagining the excitement that's ahead on tomorrow.

CHAPTER 18

Children's Day

'Children's Day' has arrived!

On this particular Sunday, Khoi and I get up without mama even having to drag us out of bed. We both get up on our own and are totally dressed before she is.

Mama calls Uncle Sherman, while buttoning Khoi's sleeves. She tells him not to pick Khoi up before church. For some reason, she insists that we all three ride together this morning.

With her acting this way, it kind of reminds me of our family portrait once more.

We reach the church's parking lot in no time. As a matter of fact, we are the first ones to arrive. Our car looks like it's packed to go on a month-long road trip.

Or else, a camping trip.

While still inside the care, mama searches for the church's spare key she still carries on her key ring. She's been having it on there every since my grandfather preached here. She flips half way through her keys before Khoi springs from the car.

"Boom!"

". . . And don't slam that car door!" mama sets out to say a second too late. My brother is always the first person out the car any where we go.

As usual, he sprints off seeking somewhere to play while she and I are just getting out of the car.

Khoi, you'd better not get dirty, either!" she demands walking toward the trunk.

She and I pull boxes from the trunk and the back seat, too. Earlier, we had to help her rearrange the trunk three times before everything could fit properly.

All Khoi ever wants to do is play, though; running through those headstones as if he's in a maze. He didn't even ask mama if she needed any help before he sent himself bolting off.

O'Peniel and a small cemetery are situated right next to each other.

I have some family members who are buried over there. Grandmommy buried Papa Joseph several years ago by the tallest magnolia tree. I've heard this magnolia tree was once O'Peniel's 'marker' before its marquee' was put up. Yep, it's another trademark as I see it.

Besides some family members, about 12 others are buried over there, too, because this was once the only burial ground Black people could use in this particular area.

Disrupting my reflections, "Rhyah, what are you gazing at over there?" mama says as she hurries toward me. She's been moving fast every since she got out of the car—alternating between going to the trunk and the back seat. Then, she'll retrace her same steps.

"This is the key to the church. The boxes over there belong in the storage room.

Please, set them in there for me."

"Yes, ma'am."

She, then, takes a single, deep breath before turning to look for Khoi. Solo breaths are something else she'll do when we reach far beyond getting on her nerves.

She spots him.

Like I expected, he's running through the cemetery—this time, jumping over headstones as if they're hurdles.

"Khoi Le Blanc!" she firmly yells. "Stop that running around and get over here and help us!"

Khoi seems to have taken one big leap to reach mama.

Briskly moving toward the other side of the car, "Go place these boxes in the kitchen," she tells him. "O.k.," Khoi responds mildly, then, takes off passing me up to reach the church's front doors first.

The key fits perfectly into the key hole. With one click to the right, the door seems to glide open causing me to reminisce about Papa Joseph again. Nudging past the corner of one of my boxes, Khoi breaks-up my thoughts.

"Hold up!" I say, careful not to lose my balance or drop any of these boxes I'm carrying.

Or, to drop mama's keys.

Or, to get my dress dirty.

Impatient, Khoi just thrusts between me and the door allowing himself to enter first. He enters the church only to run through the pews in a winding pattern. The sound of his feet and the back of his head disappear as he dashes toward the church's kitchen.

It's weird being in this quiet church without any of its members present. I've never seen it so blank in here before. Or, heard it so quiet in here.

No hoop'n and holler'n sounds coming from the pulpit.

No offbeat church songs being sang from the choir.

No waving fans.

Or, any roaring box fans for that matter.

Instead of going straight to the storage room, I head toward the front of the sanctuary.

With these boxes in my hands, I step in front of the pulpit and begin narrating the opening portion of my speech.

I imagine the pews before me as the church's members.

Pleased, I smile hearing the echoes of my words spring magnificently off O'Peniel's white walls.

Turning to leave, I notice that the crystal angel hanging in the foyer appears to have been watching me the whole time. Watching me with its entire body fully faced in my direction. Frightened, I start off by walking, but, then start running toward the back door of the sanctuary.

CHAPTER 19

Dusty Sneezes and Rubberbands

I am careful not to mess up my new dress as I enter the storage room.

Mama would otherwise never let me live it down.

Especially, on this *big day!*

I lay the boxes down right inside the storage room's entrance as Mama has instructed.

All of a sudden; I notice the tray of fans.

They mysteriously sit in a corner apart from everything else.

"So, this is where all the fans are kept?" I quietly mention to myself.

To get a better look at 'em, I instantly reach up; pulling on a long string connected to a dingy-yellow light bulb. Using dim light, they now appear even more mystifying.

"Gosh, it's dusty in here."

I am cautious not to allow anything to touch my dress, but every time I sneeze, the dust seems to spread all over me. Looking above my head, even the light bulb has dust on it.

These hand fans appear as if O'Peniel's members have been using them forever.

I say *'forever'* because they all look to be in the same worn out condition as Rev. Reeves' bible; mangled and rough.

Or, even worse like the condition of the old, worn-down carpet in his pulpit area.

On guard, I peak over my left shoulder to make sure I had not left the storage room's door open too wide. The light bulb flickers. Off it goes to only come back on again.

Then again, it goes off a second time only to immediately come back on again.

Fearful, but still interested, I begin to search among the fans.

This tray is full of fans right now.

They're 'running over' just like that verse about a cup in the Bible.

Once service has begun, however, there probably won't be *'a one'* left in this tray.

I notice the handle on this one is about to fall off.

This other one happens to be creased in *three* different ways. Its even creases seem to block out any views; from the front and both sides.

I picture myself fanning with this one as if I were Grandmommy. Its cracked handle is obviously sticking out of the tray and it sits opposite as to how the others are placed.

"Is it sitting this way for an easy-grab? Did someone place it in this position for a reason?"

Grandmommy always waves her church fan real slow and close to her face, but in a way as to never let it touch her nose.

Rummaging some more, I find that this other fan is soft along the edges. My brother must have chewed on it. He now chews on his shirts every since mama broke him up of his thumb-sucking habit. In place of his thumb, he'll take a wad of any shirt he's wearing and put it in his mouth to suck or chew on.

At times, these shirts can get really nasty!

All smelly and sticky!

Mama sometimes has to use several kinds of laundry stuff to get gum or stains out of 'em.

This is why my Uncle Sherman started calling him 'Camel'.

Daddy and my Uncle Edward picked up on Khoi's nickname and they, too, sometimes call him 'Camel'. Mama, though, named Khoi after an Asian classmate from high school. He shares the same middle name as daddy; De Lorion.

There's something about names with mama. For some reason, she seems to think someone's name will tell you all about that person.

Lipstick is all over this fan. My Aunt Lorice has probably used it at one time or another.

Oh, my goodness! This other fan has *"IT WAS GOD and NOT LUCK!"* written all over it. And the handwriting looks just like that of Aunt Gayla's when she wrote my speech.

I wonder why she'd write such a thing on a church fan.

While placing the last one back into the pile, I discover two other fans tightly connected by rubber bands.

"Rubber bands!

Why rubber bands?"

"What on Earth for?" I wonder; unless they were used for double protection.

CHAPTER 20

Sneakin' and Snoopin' Around

"R-H-Y-A-H H H H!" Shouts Khoi, from down the hallway. "Mama says where are you?"

"Coming!" I promptly answer in order for him not to come any closer.

Shuffling around some more, I find a note written to Gabriel on this fan over here. "Gabriel, meet me outside after church," it reads. Either Morgan or Kristi wrote this, I'll bet ya. Gabriel is Aunt Lorice's only grandchild and my third cousin. Or, whatever they call it when relatives start falling down the line. If it weren't for Aunt Lorice, he would never get to come to church or pretty much do anything else. When Aunt Lorice isn't busy doing her '*own thing*', she picks Gabriel up and chauffeurs him around. Her son and his wife are still separated so they pass Gabriel back and forth from one week to the next like a 'hot potato'.

This probably disturbs Aunt Lorice because she does not have any other grandchildren. 'Gabe' as she calls him, is her only one.

Mama and Aunt Gayla don't like it, either.

Aunt Gayla thinks neither one of his parents want the responsibility of taking care of him; as if he's some kind of a burden.

Personally, I think it disturbs Aunt Gayla because she does not have any children of her own yet. So, therefore, how could both of his parents be so non-caring? We all know that if it weren't for his grandmother, he would have been adopted out by some other loving couple by now.

What I ought to do is take this fan and show it to my Uncle Sherman. Mama would have my behind if she knew I had written something like this to some little boy.

I have to always stay seated in church like a bump on a log while Kristi and Morgan get to do whatever! And Paul, Jr. and Marcus get to do whatever they want, too.

"Uh, oh!" I whisper under my breath.

Distracted by yet another fan. This one has two holes poked into it. I can clearly see right through the two holes.

I am left curious as to who would have used a church fan as a *mask*?

What is so important about these fans, anyway?

Why do O'Peniel's members grab at 'em as soon as they enter the church foyer?

Even when the cold weather comes, every member will still snatch a fan.

There definitely shouldn't be a need for anyone to have to use a fan during the winter months.

"What do these church fans *really cover up*?

What do they *really hide*?"

What's *really going on* with 'em, anyway?

I ultimately wonder even as I explore yet another one.

Doesn't everyone realize that *God sees all* and you *can't hide* from Him . . . no matter what?

Khoi all of a sudden appears behind me. "RHYAH, mama says to come NOW!"

"O.k., I'm coming," I reply in a startled voice.

I instantly hold my heart due to having a sudden feeling of being saved.

Saved, because the door behind me is only partially open, so—he probably did not see me with these fans in my hand. I am glad it was not anyone else who might have seen me sneaking around in this storage room.

Hoping not to get caught again, I still can't help but to continue digging amongst the fans. This one has been folded into some type of shape.

On its backside, musical notes are drawn on it.

Bored stiff during one of Rev. Reeves' sermons, Sis. Bradley, must have done this. She's about the same age as Grandmommy with chubby fingers and little, fat feet. Mama got mad at me one Sunday because I kept asking why each of Sis. Bradley's fingers covered each key on the organ as she played.

I just did not understand why her hands appear to be filled with helium. She's a pretty lady, however, who probably could have won homecoming queen in her younger days—but, just real nosey. She's so nosey till she knows all about the church announcements or special prayer requests before they can be heard on Sunday mornings.

While trying to straighten 'em all of the fans back into some type of order, it becomes clear that they must help keep O'Peniel's members from facing their pasts and guard them against any future persecutions.

"I'd better hurry", I silently say, knowing that the congregation is beginning to fill the sanctuary. Being that it's getting closer to service time, I can hear more and more voices in the distance.

Besides, Bro. Carrington, for sure, will be coming this way soon.

Being our head deacon, he makes certain the adult congregation is well equipped with fans for O'Peniel's weekly battle on words.

Bro. Carrington will faithfully take this tray and sit it on the little, brown table in the foyer every Sunday morning. Besides, I'm sure mama's real curious as to where I am by now.

Yes, indeed. Now, I know where the fans are kept!

Before turning off the storage room's light, I begin to speculate as to what would happen if this fan tray *should 'unexpectedly' disappear* from within this room?

"What would O'Peniel's members do?
Yea. How would they react?

*Letting out a loose giggle, "Uh, huh, what would the
members say then?" I finally marvel.*

At once, I immediately remember the coat closet directly across
the hallway.

"No one will find this tray full of fans over there," I suspect.
The coat closet has not been used for months. Especially, since the
summer season is refusing to come to an end.

"Yea, the coat closet will be a great hiding place!"

It's just across the hall from the storage room. Only a few baby
steps away.

I sneak across the hallway; tiptoeing and smiling.

There are a number of cobwebs around the hinges of the coat
closet's door.

Seeing these webs reassures me that no one hasn't entered into
this room recently!

I open up its door, but look around first. Cautious, but also in
a rush, I hurry to place the fan tray under an old maroon and grey
choir robe while dodging any spiteful spiders in-between. All the
choir robes hanging up here are the older ones that O'Peniel's choir
wore when Papa Joseph was preaching. New ones were purchased
when Rev. Reeves came. He changed their color, but made it a
requirement that the older ones never be thrown away.

My Aunt Gayla thought this decision was so strange. She
persistently inquired about it in a business meeting at church one
evening. Rev. Reeves never answered her directly. But, preached
about falling by the sword due to having a sharp tongue the very
next Sunday. And of course, he preached on this subject while
pointing his bible directly in Aunt Gayla's direction.

I cautiously place the fan tray to the rear of the coat closet, on
the floor and right next to a bundle of wire coat hangers. Then, I
carefully make sure a choir robe completely covers this whole tray
of puzzling fans.

"Curiosity killed the cat, but satisfaction brought it back!" plays
through my mind before I stick my neck out the door.

Next, my eyes actively rotate in each direction to search the hallway in case anyone else is around.

Still tiptoeing, I gently close the door behind me.

"The sun is sure to shine bright today and bring plenty of warm weather for a while.

No one's going to be using this coat closet in the near future.

"NO COATS TODAY!—SO, NO CHURCH FANS TODAY!" is what I gladly figure while walking back toward the sanctuary.

CHAPTER 21

The Fan Dilemma I

"Oh! There you are, Rhyah. I was just about to come and look for you." mama calls out two pews away.

She then hurries to take her favorite end seat; the one on the fourth row, to the right of where Rev. Reeves stands—when he's facing the congregation. I take my seat next to her, as usual, to await what is to become of the *fan dilemma*.

Mama, however, never uses a hand fan while at church. She once told me that the reason she doesn't is because—no matter how much you try to push *IT* away, *IT'LL* always come back to you one day, so that's where *PRAYER* comes in!

Mama is a straightforward type of person. You'll never have to wonder where she's coming from. She doesn't wear '*rose-colored glasses.* She sees life the way it is and accepts it as is. Mama doesn't worry about the past, either. Or, about the future as far as that matters.

"Well, the program has officially begun, I guess." You see, Sis. Bradley is up there playing away at that organ to open today's service. Her soft tunes sound funny; kinda like those of an amateur musician. Maybe she can't keep focused on the organ's keys because of looking around the church and watching Bro. Carrington. He just entered the sanctuary empty handed.

(Thank God he somehow missed me. We must have been seconds apart from having missed each other back there.)

Each time Sis. Bradley looks a different way, she hits a wrong key. She catches another glimpse of him.

Her plump fingers pause long enough this time to watch him go throughout the church in search of the missing fans. Wiggling in my seat, I feel so silly inside watching them parade around. "No one knows how much I intend on enjoying church today," I mumble trying not to speak too loudly.

CHAPTER 22

The Fan Dilemma II

"Good morning, Vanessa." Uncle Edward says interrupting my concentration of today's events.

"Hello, Edward'" mama replies.

"You are growing up like a weed, Rhyah," Uncle Edward tells me pinching my cheeks.

Uncle Edward brings up the fact that there aren't any fans in the foyer. Looking worried, he takes a quick peek over both shoulders. First, over the right one to see if the fans have been returned to the foyer.

Secondly, over his left shoulder to make sure Rev. Reeves hadn't made it up to the pulpit yet.

Mama assures him that she has not even heard about any missing fans because she's been in the church's kitchen. She then goes on to tell Uncle Edward about what's going to be served after church this afternoon.

Uncle Edward, still appearing troubled about the missing fans, doesn't even listen to mama. Instead, he checks back over his left shoulder. He's not worried about any food right now, just the fact that there aren't any fans available.

"No protection for him, either, today." I say chuckling to myself.

Uncle Edward is daddy's younger brother.

Daddy does not have any sisters.

He's a good uncle. If we see him around town, he'll give Khoi and I money to buy whatever we want.

And he still calls Khoi 'Camel' just like daddy and Uncle Sherman.

"Vanessa, you're sure doing well raising these kids without Royce being around the house."

"Not without His good grace; Never without His good grace," mama proudly tells Uncle Edward.

"See ya, Rhyah."

"Bye, Uncle Edward."

Without a fan, Uncle Edward walks toward the back of the church in search of a seat. Mama said a long time ago that Uncle Edward only comes to church when things aren't going too well in his life.

Peering back over my right shoulder, I see him attempting to squeeze into one of the back pews. I sure want to laugh out loud right now, but mama; and you know how she is, wouldn't tolerate that type of behavior in church.

As I've said before, we do have another grandmother; daddy and Uncle Edward's mom.

But, we don't see or really even know her. Or, their dad; my only living grandfather.

My daddy's mother never seemed to like mama. My family suspected it because of all of the *dirty looks* she used to give mama. Somehow, I recall someone saying that my other grandmother once told mama on their wedding day, "You appear to be the type of lady who wears the pants in the family. My son will be the only man in your house. Do away with all of your pants. And put on a dress so that you will always stay in your place."

All I've ever known about my other grandfather is that Khoi and daddy supposedly look just like him. From all of the stories I've ever heard about my other grandmother is that she's like the '*bad witch*' in the storybooks.

Daddy and mama divorced when Khoi and I were about to turn 4 and 5 years old. Needless to say, mama has pretty much taken care of us since then. Well, she and Grandmommy.

CHAPTER 23

The Fan Dilemma III

Bro. Carrington, seemingly frustrated over the missing fans, has just about gone through every area of this church. He struts toward Sis. Bradley using only his hands to dramatically communicate with her—quickly moving 'em around and pointing in the direction of the congregation. If I didn't know any better, I'd have thought he was using sign language. In return, Sis. Bradley always shakes her head—to answer no.

Apparently, he didn't seek out the *coat closet*.

. . . . and thank goodness for that!

Like I said—probably, because no one will be using the coat closet today or anytime soon.

The church is full, but services still have not begun.

Some visitors have brought along their own fans since O'Peniel does not have air conditioning. I notice Uncle Edward has now moved slightly behind a tall lady. I guess he feels safe there because not only is she waving a fan, but she's wearing a large brimmed hat with two large feathers poking out of it. Obviously, she's a visitor who knew to bring along her own fan from her own church.

I can hear O'Peniel's members whispering to one another concerning the missing fans. Sis. Bradley's still misplaying the same tunes over and over; stalling for time.

Since it is 'Children's Day', the choir will not be singing. And, I'm not complaining, either. Our choir is only made up of about 5 or so women; and mostly older ones. The only music to be heard today will be that of Sis. Bradley's organ.

There are no hand fans for O'Peniel's crowd; just plenty of worried faces.

I confess! I'm getting a big kick out of all this as my eyes circle the church.

Morgan steps up to begin today's program. She tries to initiate giving the announcements even though Sis. Bradley continues to play unsteadily. Sis. Bradley is so nervous; she hasn't even realized that the program has begun or that someone's trying to speak over her inconsistent tunes.

"Today's announcements are . . ." Morgan yells into the congregation.

She's reading loud and fast to get everything all read. She has to do this or she won't be heard over that organ.

I kinda feel sorry for Morgan, but whatever . . . ! "This is what she gets for being mean to me in the past." I say to myself.

Controlled chaos is a better way to describe this entire scene.

With Sis. Bradley now playing the organ at full volume and Bro. Carrington pacing in front of Morgan, no one else seems to be paying Morgan any attention, either. "Goody for her", I taunt, "I'm the star of the show, anyway." Everyone, except mama and I are worried about the missing church fans. Just like Uncle Edward, others have begun to shift around in the pews in search of 'seats of safety'.

Kristi then walks up to begin greeting the congregation. It's funny how quickly she just had to jump out of Bro. Carrington's way twice before taking her position. Without giving an expression, "Good for her, too!" I mock.

She, too, has to begin speaking loudly to be heard over the organ.

Kristi stops speaking.

Then, starts-up again.

She looks over her eyeglasses at Uncle Sherman in uncertainty.

Confused, "Is it my turn now?" her lips ask my Uncle Sherman.

With anxiety written all over his face, my uncle beckons for her to continue speaking.

Apparently, she's unsure if it's really her turn—all because Bro. Carrington, large and hefty as he is, keeps strolling in front of her. His butt alone hides most of her body; not to mention the loud music that's going on behind her.

She's messing up on today's greeting and I'm enjoying every bit of it. For once, Kristi and Morgan are being humiliated. Payback!—for all of the nasty remarks they've made to me in the past.

Kristi, still frustrated, tries to get more words out, "Today, we welcome you to—."

But, is unable to complete her sentence due to a distraction near the foyer.

It's Bro. Carrington, again. He's motioning to all deacons that he cannot find the fan tray. He desperately rechecks with each of 'em—including Bro. Campbell.

Totally amused, all I can do is quietly laugh inside.

With a baffled look, "Please take the time to meet . . . Kristi pauses before trying to continue . . . our pastor after church . . .".

Again, unable to finish, Kristi becomes distracted by Bro. Carrington yet again who is now circling the entire pulpit area.

As it is, he is stopping on each side of her; taking glances at the whole congregation to see if any of O'Peniel's members have begun to wave one of our own hand fans yet.

"Nope!

No one's located 'em," I say giggling from within all over again.

O.K.

I am really trying not to laugh harder covering my mouth and all, but it's amusing seeing our church members' faces. Their eyes seem to be crying out, 'Save us!' 'Save us!' each time Bro. Carrington whisks by. Or else, when someone gazes toward that foyer.

Kristi, all fed up, leaves to take her seat alongside Morgan.

With a chilled feeling, "No use!" I confess watching her shamefully sit back down.

Just like Morgan, Kristi was a disaster, too.

"Goody, goody, gooodyyy. Ah ha, ah ha ha! Now, ya'll see how it feels to have your feelings stepped on," My eyes tell the both of them.

"Rhyah, take your hand away from your mouth. Are you chewing gum?" Grandmommy bends back to ask in between watching all of the charades.

"No, ma'am."

Mama having overheard Grandmommy uses one eye to peak down at my mouth when she thinks I'm not paying attention.

". . . and sit up!" mama says catching me slumping so that I won't burst out with laughter.

CHAPTER 24

The Fan Dilemma IV

A few members are leaving their seats to request additional copies of today's program from the closest usher they can find.

Instead of only accepting one; some people are asking for two or three of 'em. One usher, Sis. Pearl, on the other side of the church, seems to be handing out extras even without a request. Stepping on toes to reach peoples' hands, "I have extras. I have plenty. Ya'll take these," she insists.

I see Mrs. Carrington creasing another program as she looks toward Rev. Reeves' study. She's Bro. Carrington's wife, so I know she's feeling her husband's pain.

"Ha!"

This is better than being at the movies. Live action playing out before me. Drama and suspense, too. Everything is right before my own eyes."

Rev. Reeves came out a little while ago and went back in. I guess, figuring today's program was running behind schedule. Anyway, to prevent anyone from seeing her make a fan out of church programs, Mrs. Carrington has her bible propped up in her lap.

"I see her, though." Yes, indeed. I don't miss anything. I can clearly see what she's doing. All I have to do is move forward a bit in my seat and raise my back away from the pew. Look at her: over there pretending to be folding and licking one of those tithing envelopes, but I, for sure, know what she's trying to do. She's trying to hide!

Uh huh, my eyes tell no lies.

And she's even formed a handle to it.

"Now how she did this?—I have no idea!"

She'll only raise her head every so often to see if anyone else is noticing. Or, to make sure Rev. Reeves is still in his study.

Half smiling, again, "Nobody, but me!" I reposition my body to assume. "No one but I knows where those fans are today!"

"Rhyah, girl, don't start that fidgeting!

Church has not even really begun and you've already started up.

And what are you looking around for?

Be still!

I'm not having that today!" mama swiftly blares in my right ear.

It's apparent to me that O'Peniel had used those paper and wooden objects as ornaments of protection for way too long.

CHAPTER 25

A Test of Faith

Rev. Reeves exits his study again. But this time, he anxiously approaches the pulpit looking at his watch. He interrupts Khoi's opening prayer before my brother can end it his own self. Rev. Reeves interrupts to give a loud and quick 'Amen'.

"That's o.k," I use my eyes once more to tell Khoi.

I love my brother. I do.

When stuff happens to him, I blame daddy. If daddy were around, then Khoi, I think, would be not be as silly as he is and be more mature like me since mama, a female, is always around.

Standing tall, Rev. Reeves turns toward Sis. Bradley. He frowns at her which finally brings the music to a halt.

The marquee' reads that today's sermon is titled 'Annual Children's Day Program: Teach A Child In The Manner It Should Go."

"Set examples that can only be productive for your children," is the first phrase of Rev. Reeves' sermon that he throws at the congregation.

Necks stiffen.

Bodies harden.

And church members' faces still appear troubled.

No one moves while waiting to see who Rev. Reeves' next victim will be this morning.

By the way, all members who arrive late, motion to Sis. Pearl about the missing fans tray. She always answers back, though, with a dull look. A dull look of confusion with a short shrug of the shoulders is how I can best describe her responses.

Bro. Carrington finally gives up on looking for the hand fans or their tray.

He takes a seat next to the foyer, not along the sidewall with all the other deacons, as he normally does. Today, he sits there on the edge of his seat keeping watch on the foyer as if those fans are going to magically reappear somehow.

Rev. Reeves is knocking that bible around. Just listen to him. Screaming and carrying on up there as he preaches. He doesn't seem to be wasting any time today in search of his prey.

"Why does he shout like that all the time, mama?"

"Oh, my goodness . . . Rhyah, *don't! start*, please!" she quickly responds.

Then, she rolls her head and neck back around before twitching her body.

"It takes a whole village to raise a child," he hollers.

Tension fills the air! Clouds of anxiety hover over the pews like low-lying fog in the Louisiana springtime.

You can almost feel the strain of pressure rising! . . . See it, too!

Members aren't focusing on the sermon, but are still distracted by the missing fan tray that has always been there for them in the foyer.

Aunt Norice is fidgeting. She's trying to make herself a fan out of two programs once she notices how effective Mrs. Carrington's is.

Minus a fan, Grandmommy has not looked near the pulpit since Khoi attempted to open up today's program up with his morning prayer.

I see that Uncle Sherman is not looking up, either.

He's pretending to be taking notes of the sermon on a tithing envelope.

Aunt Gayla, desperate, finds a copy of my speech in her purse. And with no time to spare, she quickly (and neatly) folds the speech in half and begins to wave it like a fan.

"Parents must be aware of their actions! Children's minds are like video recorders!

A family that prays together, stays together!" he boldly preaches while switching his focus onto mama.

Mama's tightly folded arms begin to loosen and fall into her lap. Her head drops back without showing any emotion.

"Oh, No!" Rev. Reeves is singling mama out this time and she does not even have a hand fan!

I have to go get her one!

While attempting to ease away, mama catches the tail-end of my new dress and asks, "Where are you going?"

"To the restroom." I reply.

"Wait until he finishes preaching!" she whispers to redirect me.

Then, gives me one of her unique looks. But this time, she does not roll her head and neck because Rev. Reeves then shouts, "Parents choose to walk away from their commitments; leaving innocent children to be minus one parent."

"Oh! No! I can't believe this!" I mumble to myself.

He isn't wasting any time to score victims today.

But, is he trying to refer to daddy, too?

In anguish, "I don't understand!" I say to myself.

Why does he keep screaming *parents*? Mama is just one person—not two people.

Oh, my goodness. Who all is Rev. Reeves talking about?

Mama?

Daddy?

Mama *and* Daddy?

Mama's once crossed legs are now set apart and her light brown eyes seem to be flashing back at him.

"I know he's not trying to test my faith!" mama lets escape beneath her breath.

"School teachers are not their parents.

YOU ARE!" he continues to jeer with his eyes still glued to mama.

After looking at Khoi and I, mama begins to gently tap her foot.

"You walk around here complaining about things that are blessings from God . . . Complaining about this . . . Complaining about that!

You have a loaf of bread right under your arms, but yet, you still complain about how the butter tastes.

STOP! . . . And recognize the blessings God has bestowed upon you!

STOP! . . . And just be thankful!

. . . . JUST BE THANKFUL!

Straight and direct, Rev. Reeves hurls these words in our direction.

At no time did I move again. I better not had. Mama or Grandmommy would have had my behind. Not to mention Aunt Gayla. She would have made me practice sitting up at church for the rest of my life.

"But, what does he mean by all of this?" I begin to speculate as he goes on with his war of words.

I can only question whether he overheard Uncle Edward and mama's conversation on her having to basically raise us single handedly. Rev. Reeves did leave his study earlier and then return to it. Could he have overheard their discussion before stepping back into his study?

"But, daddy is not here. Why would Rev. Reeves refer to him in today's short sermon?"

"Oh! That's right!" I finally figure.

"Uncle Edward is here, so Rev. Reeves must be trying to send *a message* to daddy through him."

Mama's still lightly tapping her foot, but other than that, she continues to show no emotion.

If only I had not hidden the fan tray, mama would have some protection right now.

This is my fault.

This is a-l-l my entire fault!

Mama is left without anything to soften her blows!

And it's all because of me.

In an attempt to end his sermon, he slams the palm of his hands on both sides of the pulpit and then finalizes it all with a dreadful look at mama.

Before taking his seat, he forces out one last phrase:

"STOP . . . before your children become, yet, another statistic!"

CHAPTER 26

Motionless

I had totally forgotten it was 'Children's Day' until Rev. Reeves calls for me to come on up. He was seated, but makes an obvious attempt to stand back up. This time to make stronger eye contact with mama—(all while pretending to be waiting on me to approach the front of the congregation).

Motionless mama remains.

Rock-solid.

Unmoved by his apparent acts of intimidation, she keeps her eyes cemented on him, as well. I knew Rev. Reeves was not going to preach long with it being Children's Day and all, but I never expected this.

Never . . .

Never would I have thought he would have attacked my mama and daddy.

Once I begin to get up, it's only then that mama decides to budge.

"Go ahead, honey. It's your time to shine." Mama softly speaks to me.

She pats me on my shoulder giving extra assurance.

I rise up confident.

But yet, I do feel a bit responsible for the misery I'm placing on O'Peniel's members.

. . . and the misery I've probably placed on mama, too, for having hidden the fans.

"The members' flustered actions and worried faces; something that I've caused.

And more over, Rev. Reeves' attempts to bully mama." I remind myself stepping over mama's feet.

. . . And I'm about to have to face these people, too. These same people who I've made feel insecure."

My heightened feelings of excitement begin to collapse.

Aunt Gayla mouths the introduction of my speech to me as I turn to look toward the congregation.

All of a sudden, my entire mind goes blank.

Blank as an old, dried up swamp bed.

Brain-dead and hollow.

Lifeless, I am feeling.

Empty.

Just, plain empty.

Senselessly empty, too—to the point I am totally thoughtless and can't remember any parts of my speech.

"Aunt Gayla and I have rehearsed this speech so many times", I tell myself, trying to recall it. O'Peniel's members and visitors await any sounds to come out of me.

But, nothing.

Nothing comes out.

Then, I see mama.

She's still sitting there all neat; totally still—with no expression.

All eyes remain on me.

My body becomes more rigid.

For some reason, I just cannot stop thinking about Rev. Reeves hammering mama down moments ago or the chaos I have just caused in church today. I'm all iced-down and don't know what to do until mama beckons for me to come back to my seat.

I hear Bro. Campbell along with some other people saying, "Amen."

Grandmommy, in a low undertone, says, "That's alright, baby!" on my way to sit back down. Upon reaching my seat, mama grabs my hand and lifts my hanging head. She strokes my back to give comfort. It feels like my guardian angel has just appeared in mama's body.

No church fan could have ever saved me the way she just did.

Once services end, mama and I walk straight to her car.

I did notice she was gathering her purse and keys before the benediction, but I didn't know that she was planning to leave this early.

Taking big steps in order to keep up with her, "Mama, why are we leaving so early?

We haven't eaten yet?"

Mama ignores me.

"Mama, didn't you have to help serve dinner plates today after church?"

Knowing that it'll be hard not to pay me any attention, she finally mentions, "I didn't feel like staying to talk to anyone after church or to help serve dinner plates this afternoon."

"Rhyah, close the car door, please. Let's go."

She looks over in the direction of Papa Joseph's headstone and slowly begins to drive out of the church's parking lot.

"Oh! Wait a minute! Didn't you have to go to the restroom earlier?"

"Uh, uh. Yes, mam, but I can wait."

"Mama, why did church start so late today?"

"I heard they were looking for the fan tray, Rhyah."

"Well, where was it?" I further inquire, fishing for answers.

"They never found it, but your Grandmommy told me just last week that a new cleaning lady had started working for the church. So, I figure she's probably misplaced it for the moment."

I took two sighs of relief; realizing that no one had suspected me.

CHAPTER 27

A Traveling Mind

Mama's still driving slowly. She's also rubbing both knees.

"Are you alright, mama?"

"Yes, Rhyah. Sometimes I just get a little sluggish, that's all."

After that, she quickly changes the conversation to say, "Let's stop by Ms. Carolyn's house so that you can use the restroom. We can't be long, though, because Sherman will be dropping Khoi off at home soon."

I, however, know my Uncle Sherman like the back of my hand.

He'll be at church a while, at least. He has to eat, and then run his mouth; all while Khoi and the other kids get to play all up in and outside that church house.

"Mama, why did Uncle Sherman marry someone who had a bunch of kids already? Especially, since he does not have any of his own?"

Looking at me strangely, "I don't know," she answers.

"Well, why do her sons and daughters have several different last names? Both Paul, Jr. and Kristi share the same last name while Morgan and Marcus use (two) other different ones—ones that are unlike each of their siblings'.

And before marrying Uncle Sherman, Aunt Margie's last name didn't match either of theirs, either."

"Huh?

Huh, mama?

Why, mama?" I impatiently ask once more.

"Rhyah Ann, your little mind travels from one thing to the next, doesn't it?" she adds grinning and shaking her head.

"You are *so inquisitive!*"

"What's in-, in- . . . ?"

"Inquisitive!! mama reiterates with a little umph in her voice. What's inquisitive mean?" mama then asks.

"Yes, ma'am"

"'Nosey' is what it means in your case."

"Well, mama, I've often wondered about all of this. Plus, she doesn't come around our family that often . . . And then again, at Aunt Norice's last 4th of July party, I overheard her tell Uncle Sherman that our family is made up of '*educated-fools*'!"

Mama's eyes turn away from the red dirt road to give me a staggering look.

"How at the same time can a person be educated and a fool, too, mama?" I continue questioning her without even leaving room for any answers.

". . . and . . . and . . . mama, I overheard Aunt Margie bring up Rev. Reeves' name during that same point in time. She said he gets his *spiritual pride* by cutting other people down.

Some of the stuff he preaches about may be true, as Aunt Margie explained it, but did it have to be thrown back into people's faces.

Plus, mama, she mentioned how he stands behind that pulpit supposedly preaching the gospel, but, in turn, he's really ridiculing the congregation for its downfalls.

And . . . and . . . how he acts holier than 'Thou' when he's in public.

Aunt Margie further told my Uncle Sherman that no one knows what kind of past Rev. Reeves left up North before moving down here to southern Louisiana.

I heard her, mama. Yep. I heard it all at that 4th of July party.

"Was he running from something up there?" Aunt Margie kept mentioning to Uncle Sherman that day.

Did he, himself, possibly leave a secret behind?" she bravely advised Uncle Sherman. Mama, do you know Uncle Sherman never responded. He just stared at her . . . much in the same way you're staring at me right now.

Yes, mama and I saw and heard it all from within Aunt Norice's kitchen!

Mama, Aunt Margie even spoke about Rev. Reeves being some kind of a sheep in wolves clothing. I didn't really understand that, though, because how can a sheep put on clothes? . . . And a wolf's outfit at that? Or, better yet, why would she compare Rev. Reeves to animals?

I really became confused when Aunt Margie talked about him ga . . . galli . . . *gallivanting* around town claiming to be *doing good deeds*, but really *spying in secret.*"

"What does gallivanting mean, anyway, mama?" I ask before breaking to catch my breath.

Mama has ignored all my questions up to this point and can barely concentrate on driving. After having heard all of this, her mind seems to drift. Sorta like mine does when I'm daydreaming. She keeps crossing over the white, road stripes now that we've left the black top and made it onto the high way. She almost sideswipes a guardrail once she notices that we've missed the exit to Ms. Caroline's house.

"Mama, why aren't you answering me?"

Making a u-turn, she realizes that I'll just continue to press on and eventually says, "Well, Rhyah, Margie may be a little angry about certain things in life.

She may even be a bit anti-social at times.

She has not had too many career opportunities and does not have a high school diploma. She's a hard worker, nonetheless."

"That's why education should be a high priority for you and your brother," she stresses gripping the steering wheel.

She's driving even slower now. Her only actions are to reposition her seatbelt straps along her chest and waist.

Mama appears to be reflecting on something as we barely move down Ms. Caroline's street.

Out of nowhere, she unexpectedly states, "It was a constant struggle for Margie till she met Sherman, Rhyah. But, he loves her and that's what's important,"

She mentions this in a way at coming to grips with some of her own concerns about their marriage.

CHAPTER 28

No More Tears

We pull into Ms. Carolyn's driveway; right to the rear of her long, outdated Cadillac. It's light blue in color. So are her house-shutters, her front porch, and her partially leaning fence.

The bumper sticker on the rear of her car says "Mine, 'Cause It's Paid For!"

Ricki, her cold-black Chihuahua, sprints from under the carport to greet us on my side of the car. Her other three dogs always stay tied up on the other side of the house.

Ricki is the only dog that receives special treatment. On top of that, he's the only dog that she allows in her house, too.

Ms. Carolyn has a lot of flowerbeds and thick shrubs in her front yard.

Her tall trees kind of look like the ones in the rain forests I studied in school last year. They're big and full enough to give the whole yard shade. Mama and I are careful not to step on Ricki while moving back these tree limbs along her narrow walkway. She has that green carpet that can either be used inside or outside the house laid out.

Potted plants that line up according to height direct us right up to her porch.

Ricki has a sharp, little bark. The other dogs bark as if they're about to break loose of their chains. Mama takes a seat on the front porch while I begin to knock real hard.

The only chair she's able to sit in is farthest from Ms. Caroline's front door.

All the other chairs have potted plants nestled in 'em.

People who visit her have to knock firmly. Ms. Carolyn keeps her TV turned up real loud. Plus, her dogs bark constantly.

Hearing those dogs' growl brings back some ol' memories:

Ms. Caroline had to baby sit us one day for mama. This was a while back. Khoi mainly played outside that whole day. I didn't go outside until the ice cream man was about to pass her house.

Ms. Caroline was busy in the house doing something—cooking, I think.

Khoi knew that those three dogs stay tied up outside, so, neither one of 'em would be able to catch him as he kicked at 'em and then ran away.

Well, Khoi, bored to death, kicked one of those guard dogs a little too hard one time and accidentally injured its hind leg. He then blamed the entire event on me soon after Ms. Caroline went outside to feed 'em. Ms. Caroline found that dog slumped over and twisted in its own chain.

I caught a whipping from Ms. Carolyn and mama, too. Emergency Animal Care had to come to her house to assist the dog. Before-hand, not knowing what was wrong with it, Ms. Caroline was too afraid to move him.

I'll always remember how that poor dog's bark turned into a sound only a whining child could make. That dog couldn't completely stand up because its leg was in terrible pain.

Even after the dog had been treated by animal care, all that poor dog could do for the remainder of the day was lie down and whimper.

In the meantime, I was determined to make Khoi suffer for the lie he'd told on me.

To get back at him, I told him that he had been adopted at birth. Mama scolded me and made me apologize to him. I *did* and he still *didn't* believe me—apologizing wasn't reassuring enough for Khoi. Mama had to keep telling him over and over that we were both her natural-born children. This went on for almost a week, but he still didn't believe her. Quite troubled, his small crying spells were now turning into episodes.

Eventually, mama had to pull out old (newborn) baby photos that showed her holding him.

That didn't work.

My brother just looked at the pictures with no reverse of feelings.

Then, he came to a conclusion that *his real mother* had most likely handed him over to mama at the hospital.

She found his sonogram pictures from when she was over 7 months pregnant thinking this would influence him.

That didn't work, either.

Khoi, on the other hand, proclaimed the sonogram pictures were really some other woman's baby.

Mama went so far as to let him examine his own birth certificate. She even pointed out details concerning both she and daddy.

Even then, he couldn't be swayed.

He accused her of altering it in order to place she and daddy's personal information on it.

Khoi was still not convinced and continued to question mama. It seemed mama had said all she could in order to convince my brother that he was really her son.

During that time, each and every shirt he wore stayed messy and wet in the front.

He really alarmed mama when he presented a letter to her one morning before school.

He placed it in her bedroom while she was in the kitchen making breakfast. She found it lying on her pillow wet from his teardrops. Those tears spoke for the pain in his heart. I read the letter as he began to cry again in her arms. It was a letter written to mama and basically it requested for her to help him find his 'real parents'.

I know what I said was wrong, but paying him back like that seemed to only serve him right. Mama didn't know what else to do or say to otherwise persuade my brother; as his turmoil was beginning to linger into another week. I admit, as time went on, I was kind of starting to feel sad for him just as mama had been feeling.

It wasn't until Grandmommy sat down with him that these episodes came to an end. She pressed his hands in between hers while sitting in the living room next to our family portrait.

"Baby," she spoke in an easygoing manner, "I am a witness to your birth and your Grandmommy wouldn't lie to you about something this special."

I remember her telling him that she was in the delivery room when he was born.

She described in detail how she stood opposite daddy while holding mama's hand.

How he came out yellow as the golden sun . . .

How he immediately cried . . .

How she went along with the nurses to watch him get cleaned up . . .

How he stuck his own thumb in his mouth, even as a newborn.

She had his attention for sure then, once she'd mentioned that thumb.

Following this, a grin emerged upon Khoi's tearful face. She continued telling him, "I held your little body in my arms kissing you even as you tried to sleep. And you are that very same child today; only much older, than you were then". Grandmommy, being the guidepost that she is, then removed both of her hands from around his to caress his cheeks and dry his wet eyes.

"Oh, and I'll never forget that cute, little birthmark on your bottom" she added.

Khoi blushed when she described the 'banana-shaped' birthmark located on his left hip.

Surprised, "How'd you know about that, Grandmommy?" he pressed in a somber voice.

Her only reply—a kiss to one of his damp cheeks.

From then on, Khoi was all right.

There weren't any more tears about being adopted.

Not to mention, anymore questions, either.

Looking back on this now—it was kind of funny seeing my brother so upset!

CHAPTER 29

Teacakes, s's and z's

"Rhyah Ann, why did you all of a sudden stop knocking?

And what are you laughing about? Girllll, sometimes I wish I could go inside your head?

Knock again!" mama expresses in agitation.

Then, she adjusts the ivy leaves that hang along the edges of Ms. Carolyn's front window. Still unable to see clearly, mama has to move 'em completely out of her way.

Eventually, she turns backward in the chair to peak through Ms. Carolyn's hurricane shutters.

"She's here, Rhyah. I see that her TV is on. Knock a little harder."

"Mama, I am beating as hard as I can."

Before my knuckles begin to bleed, Ms. Carolyn, at last, answers the door.

She lets Ricki in first.

We then follow.

Her TV in the den is blaring!

"Rhyah, gimme a tis'," she says and subsequently wraps her arms around my head.

"Where yo' Irish twin?"

Rubbing my aching knuckles, "With my Uncle Sherman," I reply.

"Hey dere, 'Nessa. Ya'll jus' cumin' from church, yea? . . . Surprized ya'll out dis early, fo' sho.'"

Hiding the fact that Rev. Reeves had tried to torture her, "Yes, I was sort of tired, so we left a little early." Mama responds before removing a stack of old newspapers from a chair in Ms. Carolyn's breakfast room.

Ms. Carolyn then tells me to go turn down the TV in her den. She keeps the volume up loud. Surely, she doesn't want to miss her TV shows if she's in another room or if her guard dogs are barking while she's working in her yard.

We've always begged mama to get us a dog, but she won't. She states a dog is just like having to take care of another child. Every kid on our street has a dog, except us. We had a guinea pig once. Grandmommy bought it for us. It died because I bathed it outside one summer afternoon. To make a long story short—it caught pneumonia. Guinea pigs do not have strong immune systems like humans, so, it couldn't fight the pneumonia off.

I remain in the den. Ms. Carolyn and mama are sitting at the breakfast table talking. Ms. Carolyn talks a lot and speaks funny. Mama told my brother and I she had what is called a lisp.

I used to think a lisp was something that you put in your mouth like false teeth.

Because of her lisp, she uses s's and z's instead of the 'th' sound in some of her words.

She speaks as if there's a whistle stuck in the back of her throat, too.

Sometimes her words even generate a little spit.

The brown, wood-paneling in her den is covered with dozens of pictures.

Most of 'em aren't even in a frame, just stuck to the walls with thumbtacks. Or, bits and pieces of clear tape that's now yellowing.

Large wall mirrors are about strung on every wall of this room. Fake ivy vines hang in baskets that dangle around each mirror's border. The mirror across from me is the one I can see mama and Ms. Carolyn through the best. Otherwise, I can use the TV to see their reflections.

Her house is kinda crowded. Pictures of Khoi and I sit on both bookshelves, on her oversized (and out-of-date) console TV, but mainly up on each wall paneling. The couch in here is brown, but the light blue, crush velvet pillows make it stand out. The love seat I'm sitting on matches the couch, only without the velvet pillows.

Along with a coffee table, three end tables (that don't match), and another shelf, Ms. Carolyn also has this ol', reclining chair fitting tightly into a corner. The recliner has been stuck in its same slanted position for a long time. Grey, electrical tape keeps its cracked fabric from further tearing. Plastic leather is what it would remind you of. You can't adjust the recliner into an upward position any longer. And if you try to, it'll tilt over backward. I know because I experienced that mishap before.

"Rhyah, 'dere is sum tea cakes in 'dere on da kitch'n counta by da frigidaire.

Go an' git sum fo' Khoi an' yo'self. Git as many as ya want ta. I ev'n sprinkl'd a lil' suga on top ov 'em befo dey'd finish bakin', too."

Without hesitation, I walk toward the kitchen stepping over groups of magazines lying on the floor. I have to enter and exit her den on this side (the side nearest the breakfast table) because an even larger pile of magazines blocks the other entryway leading directly into her kitchen.

"Gul! She is git'n so tall, yea!" Ms. Caroline sits straight up to convey to mama.

"Ya has a birsday cumin' up soon, don't ya, Rhyah? An' a party, too, I hears."

"Yes, mam," I reply, thinking (with amusement) about her lisp when she twisted up the word *birthday*.

Trying to hold-in my laughter, a smile must have given-way on my face because mama's offering me one of her 'sharp' looks.

"How ol' is ya go'n ta turn, che? . . . 18?" Ms. Carolyn chants on with a melody in her voice.

"No, mam, but I wish I were turning that ol', though."

"Oh! Rhyah, did you still have to use the restroom?"

"Oh! No, mama, I'm o.k." I answer back making a selection of the tea cakes I want.

I choose all the largest teacakes for myself. And afterwards, I choose the next to the largest ones for Khoi.

While still in her kitchen, I've already eaten one tea cake and a half of another one.

Then, I further separate my larger stack from Khoi's stack in order to wrap 'em both up separately. I do not want my stack to be confused with his stack and he eats my big ones by mistake.

After returning to the den, I cut Ms. Caroline's TV down even lower; just in time to hear another discussion get started up.

"'Nessa', ya said earlier that you's bin a lil' tied lately?

With a southern drawl and a tangled tongue, "Has ya ova-zerted ya self?" She inquires.

I try to overlook her horrible grammar. But, it's hard to, though.

It took a while, however, to get used to it. I heard Aunt Gayla mention the very same thing one day—referring to the way she pronounces her words. Situations like this would cause Aunt Gayla's flesh to crawl.

Immediately, I stop eating the other half of my tea cake. Its crunching sound is making it almost impossible for me to overhear 'em talking.

"What 'bout dem vit'mins and ern tablis?

Has ya bin takin' 'em, yea?

Has ya had ta git anotha 'B-12' shot lately?"

In my mind, "vitamins and iron tablets," I say correcting Ms. Carolyn.

Mama tries to answer, except that she's interrupted when Ms. Carolyn asks, "Is ya hongry?"

Through the TV's reflection, I see Ms. Carolyn get up to go into her kitchen.

She almost trips over Ricki's food bowl that's laying smack-dead in the middle of her kitchen floor. In a child-like voice, "Ricki, cum an' eat da res of yo' din-din," she calls out to him.

From her breakfast table to the kitchen, people have to walk sideways because again her house is full of insignificant collectables from over the years.

Nothing matches anything else in here. Instead of throwing useless items away, she continues to cram 'em into this ol' house like an inside junk yard.

"She must cherish these things, but good grief!" I tell myself staring at the buckling walls and the outdated carpet.

"'Nessa', I cook'd liva an' unyuns t'day.

Ya care fa any?"

Mama shakes her head—No.

"Ick!

Yuck!

I'm glad mama said no. Liver makes my own flesh crawl. Just seeing people even cook those fleshy, little pieces grosses me out!" I imagine, pinching the top of my nose.

Ms. Carolyn reaches for a box of aluminum foil lying near her tea cakes.

"Ize almos' bobby-Q'd t'day, but 'cided not ta," she informs the both of us.

Ms. Carolyn begins pull out a long box of heavy-duty foil to fix mama a to-go package, anyway.

She's a good cook. She can fix a 'mean' pot of crawfish etouffee. With Bay Leaves and everything. Khoi and I love her etouffee.

She and Grandmommy's cooking runs neck and neck—maybe with Ms. Carolyn's being in the lead.

She's a medium-brown skinned woman with wide hips that sway as she walks. They sorta look like water balloons that have been inserted into her backside. Her thick legs fill up her pants like overstuffed boudain. Big feet. Big hands. Hands strong enough to work a 'cane field. She's about the same complexion as my daddy just with a patch of gray sitting at the top of her head. Mama's probably Ms. Caroline's closest and only friend. We don't visit her that often, but she's still a close friend of mama's. Today, mama probably stopped by to get her mind off of Rev. Reeves. She's Catholic and goes to church faithfully on Wednesday mornings and Saturday evenings. She said she'd never turn Baptist because Baptist preachers hold services too long. "Wat 'tis it dey got to stan der an' say fo so long?" I've heard her tell mama.

Mr. Renaud, her husband, died and all of their children are grown and out of the house. She retired soon after he died of lung cancer. With all this clutter jam-packed in her house, the man probably couldn't breathe.

"Look at the time!

Better organizing her food to go, "Caroline, let me get on home. Sherman may be there waiting on us," mama hastily says.

Mama attempts to get up, however, but she uses the table as a crutch. Mama's palms lay flat on the table while she bends forward to lift herself up. She softly closes her eyes, only to reopen 'em in order to regain her balance.

Ms. Carolyn sees mama doing so and reminds her to take her pills regularly.

"Dem pills . . . take 'em, Nessa.

Ya heard me?"

Mama doesn't reply. Instead she reorganizes the bag full of liver.

We begin leaving and Ricki follows us all the way out.

Ms. Carolyn makes an effort to follow us in order to talk about her fall garden. With her plants situated so closely together, I can't tell which garden is for the fall, winter, spring or summer.

But, mama tells her she's in a hurry to get home.

Mama just didn't want to get caught up in one of Ms. Carolyn's seemingly, endless talking episodes and definitely be late for Uncle Sherman's arrival.

CHAPTER 30

Helicopter Mom

Tonight, my head is bursting with thoughts and I can't seem to fall asleep.

It is now autumn, but the typical autumn weather appears to be nowhere in sight.

With that, many Sundays have passed since my catastrophe on 'Children's Day.'

Khoi and I are about to turn another year older. We are only 1 year, 1 month, and 1 day apart. Because of this, mama has always made us celebrate our birthdays together. She recently gave-in to Khoi's request for a pool party in order to celebrate this year. I know he is going to invite a lot of people. I sure hope he doesn't invite Uncle Sherman's step-kids.

So far, the only persons I've put on my guest list are daddy and a few girls from school. Daddy has missed all of our birthday parties since having moved out of the house. Every since he and mama divorced, I can't even remember him calling to say *'Happy Birthday'* to us, either. He'll drop by from time to time, though, acting like there has not been any lost time since he's last seen us.

I know this bothers mama. I'm sure it bothers Khoi even more so. And as for me . . . well, well, I just want some more *'Hugs and play time.'*

With daddy not being around, mama becomes too overprotective, or at least, that's the way I see it. I guess she gets these kinds of ways from Grandmommy. At times, she can even go overboard!

I remember one incident in particular. It was at the first football game Khoi had ever played in. A player in a purple and white jersey was down on the ground. Come to find out, one of Khoi's teammates had gotten the wind knocked out of him during a tackle. Mama couldn't see the jersey's number, so, thinking that it might be my brother, she scaled up and then barreled over a waist high fence before running onto the field.

After she got close enough for the players to hear her on the field, she shouted, *"Get off my baby! Get off of him, NOW!"*

The referees blew their whistles.

Players of both teams took off their helmets.

Yellow flags were being thrown about.

One referee even threw a flag by mama's feet.

Because of mama, there was so much confusion on the field that day!

Besides that, Khoi's teammate was still lying on the ground. Mama marched over to the other team's player who'd caused the incident and acted as if she was going to spank his behind. I was so embarrassed. Everyone had remained calm in the bleachers except for mama. Mama will embarrass you and won't even care. To be perfectly honest, that's about the *only* time I wish I had had a church fan to cover my face with.

When she realized it wasn't Khoi lying there, she, along with my brother's coaches apologized to the referees so that Khoi's team wouldn't get penalized.

Khoi and his teammates ended up winning the game, after all. But, every time a player would hit the ground, the announcer would tease and request that mama stay seated.

"Remain seated, Ms. Le Blanc! . . . Please! Remain seated! . . . We already have enough refs on the field," the announcer would playfully broadcast over the loud speaker. I became even more embarrassed because everyone seated near us would look our way.

As you've already guessed, mama didn't care, though. Huh, her only priority was to make sure my brother came home in one piece.

Oh, yes! For sure, she can definitely be overprotective I recall as I hear falling leaves hit up against my window.

I don't even want to think about that time my brother and I got lost in Big Buster's Super Center . . . and it was back-to-school time, too. Put it like this, there were people all over the place. Clothes were scattered in aisles and shoes mislaid on their shelves from eager shoppers.

We were probably 5 and 6 years old at the time. Or was it 6 and 7? I'm not sure, but for some reason, Khoi and I decided to search for the toy department on our own and *without mama's knowledge*.

That was mistake-number-one in her rule book!

Once she'd realized we were no longer standing next to her, mama lost all control!

Ooh! Wee! She carried-on so in that store! Mama must have turned Buster's upside down looking for us. She screamed for the employees to not let any little black children out the doors until we were found.

Some of those same employees still remind us of the incident whenever we shop there.

Just as well, she has both of our life's paths charted out.

Well, at least from now till we finish college.

Mama and Aunt Gayla went to Spelman, so, in addition, they've already decided I'll be going there, too.

Khoi wants to attend Morehouse because my Uncle Sherman went there. Mama didn't dispute Khoi's choice. Her preferences as to where we attend college have already been decided.

My Grandmommy, on the other hand, *had* to go to our local Jr. College. The same one in which Uncle Leon now works. Back then, she didn't have any other alternatives. She told me this once before that back then, there weren't too many choices as to where she could further her education. It was either go to the local Jr. College here in town or not go to any college at all. She chose the Jr. College.

And it was there, that she actually met my grandfather. He had just started working there as a groundskeeper, my Grandmommy told me.

Mama is coming to tuck me into bed. It's no secret she's on her way to my room. Walking so fast; her house shoes sweep the hallway's wooden floor. I'm glad I'm already in bed even if I'm not asleep yet.

"Khoi is already asleep," she says pointing toward his room. Then, she takes my diary out of my hands face-up all while attempting to take a glimpse at what I've written for tonight. I already knew what she was about to do . . . she'll eyeball my diary while closing it reeeeaal slow . . . (Yep! That's what she's doing right now.) This is what mama will do if she's the one to put my diary away for the night. Yes, indeed . . . I know very well what she'll decide to do when she's the one to put away my diary for the night.

Auntie Gayla bought me this diary. It's the kind that does not have a lock on it; just some ribbons to tie it shut. I am sure she intended to purchase this type for the very same reason mama tries to take *sneak peeks* inside of it.

"Khoi had a tough practice this evening and he's all worn-out!

They have some hard-hitting teams to play in the upcoming weeks. He didn't even wait for me to give him his *'Hugs and Kisses'* before falling fast asleep.

Besides, you need to be asleep, too.

Good night, sleep tight, and don't forget to say your prayers!" she quickly says leaning over with a short hug and a tickly kiss.

"Love ya, mama!" I reply in the middle of a yawn.

CHAPTER 31

Time Really Doesn't Fly By

Several more weeks pass, only to bring about a few rain showers here and there.

I sure hope it doesn't rain today! It's Saturday and that would ruin all our plans for our birthday party. Nowadays, it's slightly cooler in the mornings, but the temperature climbs as the day goes on. Pretty soon, it'll be what mama calls—"gumbo cookin' weather"!

Our birthday party is set for 3:00 o'clock today.

Luckily, mama reserved a pavilion in case there's some rain.

The clock in the TV room now reads 11:50 am.

It's not quite time to leave yet, but Khoi has his canvas, duffle bag draped over his shoulder; ready to go! Normally, this bag is used for his football stuff, but not for today! Instead, he has it filled with his swimming trunks and pool gear.

The clock hanging in the kitchen climbs toward 1:00 o'clock; as does the one on the microwave oven.

Khoi keeps hauling that bag around the house, thinking that that's going to make mama leave much sooner. To the contrary, just the opposite happens. She only throws up her eyes, ignoring him; something he should recognize by now.

1:35 pm falls upon the clock on my nightstand.

Khoi has begun to get on mama's nerves and I'm, I guess, a little antsy, too.

He conveniently keeps passing her about the house carrying the duffle bag while I speculate on how much fun I intend to have.

The clock's hands on top of my dresser creep toward 2:10 pm.

We're preparing to leave for the party, but late birthday shoppers keep calling to get gift ideas from mama.

"Help place these bags in the trunk." and "Help place this food inside the car." she tells us between each phone call.

She makes sure to tell all callers not to purchase anything with a whole bunch of parts or pieces to it, . . . nothing that makes a lot of noise . . . or, nothing that runs by batteries . . . and *definitely* not anything that can cause a mess or a stain!

Mama, herself, has never bought us any of those types of items or toys.

Point blank . . . Period!

But, Grandmommy has and daddy has, too.

Mama would, otherwise, always make us choose simpler toys or games to play with.

She thought the simpler toys required less clean-up time and less overall maintenance.

2:25 pm is about to pass us by—given mama's final decree of, "You all didn't leave room on this side of the trunk for these bags of ice.

My goodness! Let me rearrange it right quick!"

2:35 pm appears on mama's dashboard as she starts the car's engine.

"Yes! Finally!" I hear Khoi murmuring in the back seat while we back out of the garage.

CHAPTER 32

The Birthday Party I

As we enter the park's grounds, "The sky looks promising," mama boasts.

Hyper with excitement, Khoi sticks his right arm out the window. His arm and the sun's angled rays seem to touch each other. In reality, he's trying to make sure mama does not overlook the big, blue pavilion sitting to the right of us.

Cherry Hill Park has the only public swimming pool in town.

The pool is located near our pavilion. Actually, it's really just behind the pavillion.

There are several private pools in town, but mama won't take us to any of 'em.

Private pools don't require lifeguards to be on duty.

Cherry Hill's pool has three life guards on duty at all times.

There are plenty of places out here to have a picnic. This is where O'Peniel's church picnic was held last year.

The football field where my brother's home-games are played was just to the left as we entered.

I take tennis lessons one summer near those huge light poles in the rear of the park. Mama, along with some other moms, often use the jogging trail that circles this entire park during Khoi's football practices.

"Mama, can I go put on my swimming trunks now?" Huge with anticipation, my brother asks her.

"I haven't finished unpacking the car yet, Khoi.

Come help me. Then, go help your sister put the streamers up . . . and after that you may go change."

Khoi puts up his blue streamers in a hurry.

You can tell, too. Some are drooping. Others aren't even arranged in any type of order.

I make sure my pink ones are being placed evenly and very neatly along the pavilion. My streamers hang from the ceiling. They also run up and down the columns reminding me of my lacy hair bows.

I hope our streamers and matching balloons can be seen clear to the other end of the park. Mama told everyone to look for 'em hanging-up out here.

Auntie Gayla and Grandmommy arrive soon after us.

"Where's Khoi?" Grandmommy inquires placing our birthday cake onto the food table.

Motioning in the opposite direction, "He's in the men's locker room changing into his swimming trunks." I inform her.

Grandmommy made our cake and of course, it's trimmed in pink and blue icing.

Just like our decorations.

Pointing back and forth, "The table cloths and balloons match perfectly, but if anymore of these helium balloons are blown up, this pavilion might just fly away," Aunt Gayla teases.

Our friends and family have just about all arrived.

The sun continues to beat down onto the park's grounds.

Not a cloud insight; only a baby blue sky as far as my eyes can tell.

The gifts are beginning to fill up the table that's closest to the pool.

The gifts in the big boxes appear to be for Khoi.

Most of the smaller ones are labeled for me.

Mama catches me holding a card up to the sunlight. Giving me one of her looks, she motions for me to get away from the gift table.

Grandmommy sees me, too, but she only laughs.

The small amount of friends I invited from school has all shown up.

Khoi seems to have invited everyone he knows; both girls and boys.

Mama invited a few of her own friends' children. They're mainly from work or church.

Knowing her, she probably did this so we'd end up with a lot more gifts.

Bro. and Mrs. Carrington have brought their three, small grandchildren.

They're much younger than Khoi and I. Mrs. Carrington keeps an eye on 'em playing near a swing set. Her other eye is on Bro. Carrington, especially, since Aunt Lorice has just arrived.

Of course, she and Gabriel arrive late. Just like to church; she's never on time. When our family throws a get-together, she's the one who always has to bring the non-essential items; such as extra desserts or additional bags of ice.

Aunt Lorice informed mama this morning that she had to get her car detailed first. Then, go to the wig shop in order to get the wig re-groomed.

From the parking lot, Gabriel zones-in on us swimming. Cherry Hill Park has an Olympic-sized swimming pool and he heads straight for it, too.

Aunt Lorice strolls up the entrance ramp wearing too much make-up and lipstick, as usual. You can clearly see her face from there to this pool.

She greets everyone at the top of her voice.

"Hey ya'll, sorry I am behind schedule!" She repeats multiple times.

Speaking so loudly, she sounds like a cheerleader using a megaphone.

With each acknowledgement, she gives big, rainbow-style waves; making sure she's not only heard, but definitely seen, too.

I think she's doing this in order to get noticed by people and for the most part, Bro. Carrington.

In order to tone Aunt Lorice down, "There's plenty of hot dogs and chips over here," Grandmommy openly announces standing in the middle of the pavilion.

Sis. Pearl is here with her twins, Kaelyn and Jaelyn.

They've already jumped in the pool. Sis. Pearl's about to join 'em when I notice what she's wearing. Or, in her case, what she should not be wearing. She has the nerve to be wearing a two-piece swimming suit. Put it like this: she reminds me of one of those Sumo wrestlers Khoi watches every Saturday morning on TV with a see through netted cover up.

CHAPTER 33

The Birthday Party II

As time passes; my friends and I get out of the pool to dance near the booming speakers. Uncle Sherman brought a jam-box that has speakers large enough to wake the dead. Using an extension cord he retrieved from the pool's supply room, he has his jam-box extending right up to the fence that surrounds the pool.

Initially, the jam-box was playing from within the pavilion. I knew he was going to have to eventually move it, though. Grandmommy can't stand *our type* of music. All she listens to is this one certain gospel station that plays jazz in the mornings. That is the only station that's programmed into her car stereo, too.

I don't know how anyone could possibly listen to jazz.

Wiping water from my face, "Slow-moving music or elevator music is what it sounds like to me. YUK!" I frown to say walking near the boom box while continuing to dry myself off.

Kristi and Morgan whisper to each other while looking at me dance to the rap beats.

I guess they want me to notice 'em talking about me. I don't care because Khoi and I always know the latest hip-hop dance moves. Besides, we always watch video countdowns on cable TV.

I have not seen either of 'em dance yet. They only stare and follow my friends and I around.

Their brothers aren't ashamed, however.

As a matter of fact, Paul, Jr., was one of my friend's dance partners on the last song.

All of a sudden, I remember that I'd invited daddy to come today. But, he hasn't shown up yet.

With high hopes, "Is daddy coming, mama?" I ask.

Without showing any concern, "I don't know," she hesitantly replies.

Then, she turns to look toward the parking lot.

Aunt Jan and Aunt Gayla are cutting our birthday cake. Aunt Gayla carefully cuts each of her pieces while Aunt Jan is mainly licking the icing from both sides of her knife.

Aunt Gayla's square pieces seem to be perfectly cut with all even edges.

The cake's icing never seems to touch her hands. She even uses a perfectly folded napkin to wipe away all extra icing.

She's so picky, I'm surprised she didn't bring along a pair of rubber gloves and an apron to protect her from getting dirty today.

I'm going to have to remember to ask mama again if Aunt Gayla has always been this way; so particular, especially, when they were growing up.

Sitting directly behind the food table is Uncle Leon and one of mama's friend's husbands. They're chatting about something called an S.A.T. Preparation Course.

Uncle Leon is carrying on about this course as if he'd invented it.

The other man appears to be bored out of his mind with their conversation. He's not interested in listening to Uncle Leon. He's basically kept his head turned the other way to eye down Aunt Gayla ever since she and Aunt Jan stood up to cut our cake.

Still ignoring Kristi and Morgan, I continue talking among my friends.

They've been watching my every move, especially when my friends and I began to dry-off again before eating.

A car door suddenly slams!

My friends and I are busy making our plates. But, in hopes that it's daddy, my head swivels around like an owl's neck.

Disappointed, I notice it's their mother who's parked near the entrance ramp. Morgan and Kristi's long and curly, wet hair still sways as they dart off to meet her. Running into the sunlight, Morgan's hair seems to even glisten a bit.

Because their mother is the bakery manager at Winn Dixie, she has to work almost every day. And due to her work schedule, Uncle Sherman usually has to take her kids anywhere they need to go. He seems to spend way more time with 'em than daddy does with us and he is not even their real father.

Bearing no gifts, their mother walks up the entrance ramp with her head turned away from the pavilion. She has Marcus to bring her a chair that's consequently placed in an area whereas no one else is sitting. Aunt Margie sits down, then, appears to take the chair and move it even farther away in order to avoid the pavilion area.

At that moment and oddly enough, I realize she's repositioned herself yet again.

"What is she doing?" I curiously ask myself. Aunt Margie has just moved her chair again nearest to the ramp that leads directly back to her car. On top of all of this, the only people I have seen her talk to so far are my Uncle Sherman and her own children.

She has not even greeted anyone else. Or, told Khoi or myself happy birthday.

She just sits there in her black uniform looking unfriendly. Every offer made to her by my Uncle Sherman to eat or drink something has been turned down so far.

By now, mostly everyone has finished eating, except for my friends and I.

Grandmommy is collecting trash near the other end of our pavilion. In this section, mama is doing the same, but with a super-sized trash bag. As she travels closer to where Aunt Margie's sitting, mama politely smiles and waves to her. Aunt Margie barely acknowledges mama's kind gestures. Following this, Aunt Margie quickly turns her head to look another direction.

Mama approaches our table to dispose of any other garbage in our table.

Before she completely passes us up, I catch her by the arm to whisper every single thing I've observed concerning Aunt Margie.

Mama responds by saying, "Margie just got off of work and is probably tired," then switches subjects to tell my friends and I, "wait a while before returning to the pool since you all have just finished eating."

Mama, for some reason, takes another glance in the direction of the parking lot and then strolls on toward another table.

CHAPTER 34

The Birthday Party III

The party is lasting longer than scheduled. That's o.k. with me because I am having so much fun. Morgan and Kristi are the only two people that have gotten on my nerves so far today. For sure, I am going to make it a point to tell mama that next year I want my party to be separate from Khoi's. That way, I can only invite whom I want; making sure Uncle Sherman's step-kids don't show up!

Small pieces of the piñata's colorful tissue paper are still flying in every direction.

A small chunk of the piñata, itself, just blew under the table near my feet.

The fence around the pool keeps most of its pieces from getting in there.

Oh! Did I mention that grandmommy chose our piñata? It was shaped into a saxophone. Probably, because she enjoys the sounds of jazz. Not a shade out of the rainbow was missing from it.

Khoi was the first person to burst the piñata open.

He did it on his first try. The candy came falling out like hailstones.

Mrs. Carrington grabbed the stick from Khoi to scoop up candy for her grandchildren. We were screaming and grabbing!

It was worse than revelers at a Mardi Gras carnival.

Marcus and Gabriel attempted to rip the packed piñata open before Khoi had his chance, but weren't successful. I don't know about Marcus because he's kind of puny.

But, Gabriel; he was strong enough to have done it on his first try.

It's only that he kept missing the piñata every time he swung at it.

Blindfolded, Gabriel would swing and miss terribly.

Aunt Lorice, using this moment as her time to shine again, was shouting,

"Get 'em, Gabe! You can do it, baby! Come on, bring Granny some candy!"

She was stationed in the middle of the piñata circle next to him screaming.

As it goes, the only person who's supposed to be in the circle is the one trying to break open the piñata at that time.

Without warning, the sun begins to flash brightly through a few clouds; making the swimming pool's water sparkle like diamonds. So, my friends and I return to the pool in order to get plenty more swim-time.

Being messy, Morgan and Kristi interrupt me as I'm climbing up to dive off the diving board. Kristi steps toward the bottom rung and flips open a new cell phone. With a flick of her wrist, the phone sprang open. Acting as if she's avoiding the sun's glare, she pretends to be dialing a number . . . "She's just trying to show it off because she's not really looking at the phone, but up at me on this diving board," I conclude. That's how I really know that she's faking. Plus, the way she smoothly popped it open and dramatically waved it below me on these stairs told me so.

Morgan, standing near the edge of the pool, slaps one hand on her hip and throws back both shoulders. With a cruel pose, "Why couldn't you remember your speech on 'Children's Day?'" she maliciously questions.

I ignore 'em; keeping in mind what mama has told me before. They both act as if they aren't going to move till I've answered 'em. In order to downplay the situation, I readjust my water goggles, spring upward into a leap and dive into the water like a professional swimmer.

Some of the friends Khoi invited to the party are currently involved in a separate swim race. Watchful of his friends, but determined to get away from Morgan and Kristi, I swim to the other end of the pool.

Aunt Norice has borrowed a stopwatch from one of the lifeguards.

She stands at the front end of the pool timing Khoi's friends to see who the winners will be. She, of course, has shown up without my Uncle Benny.

A few kids did not get any candy earlier from the piñata.

Everyone was rushing toward the middle of the circle; bumping heads and grabbing at whatever they could. So, some kids ended up with nothing. Since mama wants everyone to take something home, new winners of the swim races are given a dollar as their prize.

Morgan continues to follow me around in order to taunt me or to just be plain mean.

"Hey, Ms. Rhyah," she says partly smiling in her own silly way.

"When are you going to grow up and stop wearing all of those hair bows?

What's so special about them, anyway?" she persists.

Having overheard Morgan bothering me, mama calls for Khoi and I to come open our gifts.

As the crowd moves toward the gift table, a tall, dark figure marches toward us.

"It's Rev. Reeves!" I express to myself in dissatisfaction.

He marches up the entrance ramp and toward the pavilion like a person in the Secret Service. He's walking this way with a ray of sun pointing directly at his head.

I cannot believe what my eyes are witnessing right now!

"**Who—invited—him**?" I begin to wonder attempting to get mama's attention.

Even though I'm waving my hands similar to Aunt Lorice earlier, mama still does not notice me.

CHAPTER 35

The Birthday Party IV

The mood of the party immediately changes.

Besides me, Aunt Margie has apparently already spotted him, too.

She begins to leave real *fast*—so *fast* that she jets back down the entrance ramp once he has passed where she's sitting.

Her black apron gets caught in a crosswind and flies up and into her face.

That does not stop her, though. She only seems to gain that much more momentum as a result of it. Even worse, she didn't say good-bye to Uncle Sherman or her own kids.

The laughter and discussions over our gifts turn to whispers concerning the arrival of Rev. Reeves. The partly blue skies have now turned cloudier and grey creating an unusual light wind to cross through the pavilion. I just heard a clap of thunder in the distance, too.

Uncle Sherman races to turn off his jam-box.

He does so without taking either eye off of Rev. Reeves.

"What a sur—!" mama tries to get out, as he approaches her dressed in an all-black leisure suit. This outfit, along with the same black shoes he wears every Sunday at church.

Rev. Reeves then hands mama two envelopes.

"Thank you, Reverend," she gratefully responds. But, the shocked look upon her face is visible enough to tell otherwise.

With a rumble in his throat, "I would not have missed this for anything!" he replies. He raises his hands to block out the isolated sun ray from his eyes.

Without any explanation that sun ray just reappeared over his head again.

Afterwards, he scopes out all areas near the pavilion—even the swimming pool area.

Instantly, the crowd seems to stop all movement—waiting with expectations of his next move; just like at church.

If I am not mistaken, I know I just saw Rev. Reeves look back at the parking lot, too.

"What was he looking at?

Who was he looking for?"

I also saw mama looking over there earlier.

Why is there such a concern over the parking lot?

Once more, through those glasses, his shifty eyes automatically canvass the entire party area. Something like a high profile surveillance camera.

There's something strange about his facial expression as his eyes rotate about.

"It's like he's searching for something.

But, why?

What for?

This is only a birthday party. A birthday party *for kids*, at that!" I decide at once.

Rev. Reeves spots me.

To remain motionless is my first and only instinct! . . . like mama did when he stared her down on Children's Day.

Without another thought, my body becomes numb standing near this gift table.

Frozen.

I don't know if I'm now feeling frozen because of general fear or if it's out of shock from him having shown up today . . . sorta the same way I appeared while trying to give my speech that same Sunday.

And yet, still questioning why he has shown up *uninvited.*

Instantly, I turn back around to continue opening my gifts. I did not know what else to do to avoid that hostile gaze.

In a brutal voice, "Where's Khoi?" I overhear him asking mama and I. On purpose, I drop some gift wrapping paper so I won't have to answer.

Mama points toward the other end of the gift table. The same area in which Sis. Pearl happens to be standing in. As a matter of fact, I can tell Khoi is trying to hide, too—by using Sis. Pearl' body as his shield.

Forgetting about Khoi, Rev. Reeves' unexplained look leaves; only for it to turn into a frown.

Well, a frown mixed with a sense of disgust.

I say he's frowning because there's folded wrinkles that now wrap around his forehead. And I mention disgust because of the way his check just sunk-in taking in a shallow breath right before clearing his throat.

In an instant, he sees the type of swimwear Sis. Pearl's wearing.

Her netted over shirt can't hide that jiggling belly and thighs that look a lot like marshmallow puffs . . . and she'd just finish eating, too! Oh, my goodness, she's just plain puffy right now.

To be honest, Sis. Pearl has noticeable jelly-belly rolls even when she's dressed in her usher's uniform. Tight-fitting. No room for movement, either. *But today takes the cake!* Speaking of cake, she just ate two hot dogs, two pieces of cake, and a pile of chips.

Plus, I saw her finish-up the rest of Kaelyn's leftovers. All of Sis. Pearl's food seems to go straight from her lips to her hips.

I can only speculate at what Rev. Reeves' is thinking right now. What kind of sermon could come out of what his pivoting eyes just witnessed?

Further, at this point, people are using balloons as their shields.

They're using the pavilion's columns, too, to avoid any contact with Rev. Reeves.

Anything!

Anything they can use!

Anything they can find to use!

People are using or doing just about anything to stay clear of his sight.

Using a paper plate, Grandmommy begins to slowly fan herself.

The Carrington's have moved their lawn chairs behind the gift table. All I can see of 'em right now is their feet since the gifts are hiding their heads and bodies.

Interrupting a conversation with one of Uncle Sherman's step-boys, Uncle Leon abruptly jumps up. He gets mama's attention to tell her he's about to head to a store for more bags of ice. He passes Aunt Jan who points before opening up two coolers full of ice. Uncle Leon doesn't even pay his wife any attention. Instead, he disappears into the parking lot—using multiple vehicles as a way to duck for cover.

Aunt Gayla suddenly rises from her seat in an effort to head toward the food table.

"Anyone like anymore cake?" she timidly announces.

Her back remains turned, dodging Rev. Reeves or any possible interaction with him.

No one, but me, hears Aunt Gayla's offerings of additional cake as she stands there uselessly slicing new pieces.

CHAPTER 36

Saving Grace

It feels like *'a Sunday morning'* at O'Peniel until I see my daddy drive into the parking lot. The clouds begin to turn away as daddy parks and gets out of a truck.

He makes his way up the entrance ramp carrying one small box and a slightly larger one.

"Daddy! Daddy!" I happily shout, hurling myself at him.

He catches me; sweeping me up with his arms.

"NOW my day is complete!" I say to myself.

A feeling of life returns to my previously numb body. A feeling that temporarily erases all the blemishes of the past concerning my daddy.

"Happy 10th birthday, Rhyah," he utters preceding a big squeeze.

Khoi looks on at daddy as if he is a total stranger.

Rev. Reeves, attempting to eat, keeps missing his mouth as he monitors daddy's every move. Actually, he had to stopped eating altogether because the cake on his fork kept falling off each time he heard me scream 'daddy'!

He finally puts his fork down in order to totally concentrate on daddy and I.

Rev. Reeves' open hands become balled-up fists.

His relaxed back becomes raised.

He notices daddy hugging me again.

In an instant, Rev. Reeves carefully uses his thumb and index finger to reposition his eyeglasses. He begins to study daddy piece by piece with squinted eyes.

Those same kind of narrow eyes that an eagle would use once it's spotted it prey.

Daddy waves hello to mama. But, all she can do is focus on a dealership's white, paper-tag in the rear window of his new truck.

Mama seems to overlook daddy's presence for the rest of the party. But, keeps a close watch on Rev. Reeves, *as is everyone else.*

I open daddy's gift in front of him to find two pairs of gold, looped earrings in different sizes. What amazes me most is that daddy has the earrings wrapped in a small box. And on top of the box is a tiny picture of a *gold angel.* Throwing myself back into his arms, "Thank you, daddy!" I joyfully express.

While Rev. Reeves' eyes are still in-tow, daddy looks around to find Khoi.

Someone—Grandmommy, I think, points out that Khoi's still standing near the gift table.

He approaches Khoi and hands him his birthday gift.

Cautiously, "Happy 9th birthday, 'Camel'," daddy states.

"Thanks," Khoi replies, unenthusiastically. Khoi accepts the gift without even making eye contact with daddy. "Open it up now, Camel," daddy tells him. Khoi refuses to unwrap it; giving it to mama, instead.

He chooses to wait till he gets home, despite daddy's wishes for him to unwrap it at the party. Mama, then, places daddy's gift alongside all the other ones we've previously opened.

Daddy tries to kick off some small talk with mama, but she barely acknowledges him. Busy straightening out the gift table, "Uh ha and Uh uh," are her only replies.

Some remaining clouds and light sprinkles of rain bring about a slight drop in the temperature. This causes the lifeguards to close the pool and ultimately bring our party to an end.

"Vanessa, I'm going to take the kids home," daddy mentions to mama.

Having overheard this, I become even more excited about him having come today.

Sensing a little hesitance within my brother, mama's currently trying to convince him to ride back with us. He keeps shaking his head sideways every time she bends down to whisper something in his ear.

Khoi most likely wants to remain with her or get a ride back home with Uncle Sherman. Except that she and Aunt Gayla are going to stay a little longer to make sure the pavilion area is clean.

I don't know what she's saying to him but, a smile just leapt onto his face. She's probably promised to buy him. Maybe another video game or something. Knowing mama, this is the kind of stuff she'd do just to convince him to ride along with daddy and I.

Khoi remains quiet as we exit the park's grounds, but my mouth is moving faster than daddy's windshield wipers. I can tell Khoi is uneasy because he keeps looking out the window back at a newly formed rainbow. And, of course, suck on his T-shirt.

After all, Uncle Sherman is the only male-figure in his life. Uncle Sherman's also the only one that he sees on a regular basis. Basically, my Uncle Sherman is the only man he can depend on. A shrug of the shoulder is the only response daddy gets from Khoi whenever he speaks to him.

I, on the other hand, try to take advantage of this short time with him.

"Daddy, when did you get this new truck?

What are all those lights and little buttons used for up there?" I question while watching him fiddle with 'em.

"Can we ride around till it gets dark?

Take us back down the big hill near the park so that our stomachs can drop again, P-L-E-E-E-A-S-E!

What have you been doing lately? I ask him entering our neighborhood.

I'm still on the honor roll, daddy.

Oh! Daddy, will you buy me a cell phone for Christmas?

All of my friends have 'em.

Oh, Yea! Can you take us to school on Monday in your new truck instead of mama?"

Pulling near our home, "Rhyah, you're still the same," he playfully says taking a glance at Khoi through his rearview mirror.

Daddy used to call me 'Cricket' because I always moved around and made so much noise. It was the nickname he gave me around the time I learned to walk and talk, but it never stuck. The only name I ever hear now is Rhyah; the name I was born with.

Or, "Rhyah Ann", whenever mama's trying to get a point over to me. I'm going to ask her one day how she came up with the spelling of my first name. Weirdly enough, it's supposed to be African for a little girl who sparkles. Remember, I told you mama loves names. She almost named me 'River', but Grandmommy told her not to do that to me.

My middle name, 'Ann,' is also mama's and Grandmommy's middle names.

Four generations of 'Ann's' exist because my great-grandmother's middle name was also 'Ann'.

Enough already!

I am going to break this 'middle-name cycle' if I ever have a little girl. There are enough "Ann's" in this family already.

Enough is enough! . . . and to think my first name was almost named 'River', too.

'River Ann'.

Gross!!!

Uncle Sherman's step kids would surely be teasing me, then.

"You want salt and pepper to go with that T-shirt, 'Camel'?" Daddy questions Khoi, trying to get a smile out of him any way he can.

"Well, we're here. I'll be sure to call you guys early next week, o.k.".

"Come on. Let me help you two down out of the truck."

Daddy, then, makes a funny face as if Khoi and I both weigh a ton. He's not really struggling, though.

No, indeed!

My daddy has strong arms and shoulders. His wide chest matches his tall, solid frame.

"Daddy, I have not seen that face in a long time.

I remember all of the funny faces you used to make at us.

With attempts to prolong his visit, "They used to crack me up."
I amusingly tell him.

Khoi isn't interested in any of daddy's playful ways.

He walks straight into the house after retrieving our spare key.
Mama keeps it hidden under a fake brick among the front hedges.

I, though, laugh so hard at his comical faces; the misty rain
seems to stop falling.

CHAPTER 37

Speed Racer

It's the middle of next week and daddy still hasn't called like he promised he would. My mind is wandering. I barely can concentrate on my homework while sitting at my desk.

Through my bedroom's front window, I see Khoi and his friends playing 'touch-football' in the street. Khoi didn't have football practice tonight.

It was rescheduled due to the coaches getting together to review a video of another team's play-strategies.

'Screeech!'

Distracted yet again by car brakes, I raise my head to look back out the window.

I see Grandmommy pulling up in front of our house; just barely missing Khoi and his friends playing in the streets.

Before coming to a complete stop, she motions for Khoi to come over to her car.

He rushes toward her to help carry a small bag.

Aiming toward our front door, "Mammmma, Grandmommy's here!" I yell throughout the house.

On Wednesdays, Grandmommy usually goes to *The Bazaar* before she heads to *B.T.U.* church service. New items are only put out at *The Bazaar* on Wednesdays. It is located downtown in a two-story warehouse-type building. This building was once a printing company, but now it's our town's only flea market. Mama,

Khoi and I visited *The Bazaar* when it initially opened. Mama said she'd never go back, however!

First of all, the owners followed us around every time we moved from one aisle to another. *"You like, you buy."* They kept telling us.

Khoi picked up a toy. He was looking at it when one of the owners began to gravitate alongside him like a huge magnet.

Another owner told mama, *"If he break, you pay"*, using an accent in broken English. Mama got so upset, she put all of the items she was carrying down and we walked out.

Grandmommy's in such a hurry, she stops half way down the sidewalk; never completely making it into our house. Khoi hands Grandmommy the bag he's been holding for her.

". . . . coming from The Bazaar . . . to church," she states in a blur without even taking a breath.

"Rhyah, here's a pair of those curly hair ribbons. Hope you like them. Khoi, I saw this leather belt and had to get it for you," she rushes to tell us. "Thank you, Grandmommy," Khoi states as mama catches up with us on the sidewalk. I give Grandmommy a smile as my thank you. Hooked onto Khoi's belt buckle are two identical, sterling silver bracelets. "This bracelet's for you, Vanessa, and this other one's for Gayla Marie." She hands mama hers, then, unhooks the other one from Khoi's belt buckle and drops it back into the bag.

"Vanessa, I have got to go or I'll be late for B.T.U." she says, rushing back toward her car. Next, she blows her horn for Khoi and his friends to move out of her way!

Grandmommy pulls off like the bad guy in a 'getaway movie'.

Moving fast and not paying attention, her bible has fallen out of her car.

It fell out while she was fastening her seatbelt and closing her car door at the same time.

Now, it lay sprawled in the middle of the street.

Khoi's friend, Chadd, safely brings Grandmommy's bible to mama.

She grins and thanks Chadd before labeling him a "good lil' Samaritan."

With the bible lying open-faced in mama's hands, she turns its front cover.

"(**B.**)ible. (**T.**)humpers. (**U.**)nited." I hear coming from underneath her breath.

She follows a list of names and dates from left to right with her pale finger.

Peaking from beneath her arm, I realize these are all of Grandmommy's children's and grandchildren's names and birthdates. Mama's finger is zig-zagging down the front cover really, really fast. I didn't see any of Uncle Sherman's step kids' names in it.

"Good! . . . because they're really not related to us, anyway." Why would their names be in *my* Grandmommy's bible? They are in our family because of Uncle Sherman's choice.

Mama also quickly scans over a scripture; **Genesis 32: 22-32**, written just below all names and birthdates.

"Mama, why did Grandmommy write that scripture in her bible?

Is that her favorite scripture? . . . Or, is it because . . . ?" Before I can completely ask another question, mama cuts me off to say, "My mama and daddy put this scripture inside both of their bible covers because it has an impact on the meaning of our church's original name."

"What?

What, mama?

What name?" I push forward asking in confusion.

Mama seems to be in a deep state of thought by now.

But, questions are forming too quickly in my mind. I can't even hold 'em inside. As she stands there continuing to flip through the bible, I even try to remind her of what she previously mumbled to herself.

"What did you call out earlier, mama?

"Bible who?

United what?"

Mama tries to avoid my questions again, but, then boldly reveals, "Bible! Thumpers! United!" in a rather roughed-up voice.

She reluctantly lets this slip while trying to mimic Rev. Reeves' tone.

Without notice, she instantly takes Grandmommy's bible and propels it about, as only he would do in church. With the bible now raised high above her head, she starts jumping up and down like an Indian chief conducting a pow-wow! She's roaring other phrases in a manner that only Rev. Reeves could.

Still hopping up and down on each foot, "Choose Heaven, *YOU SINNERS*, not hell!" she goes on to rave.

This, in turn, leads to her whirling her body around in uneven circles.

"Save your soul! Don't forfeit it!" she rants, thumpin' and shakin' Grandmommy's bible like a tambourine.

Following her wild rampage, we both begin laughing even as we make our way back into the house.

Khoi and his friends stop playing football, at once, to gaze our way—curious as to what in a bible could be so humorous.

CHAPTER 38

5, 10, 15 Minutes

Thursday night rolls around and still no sign of daddy. No calls, either, as he'd reassured. I don't know why this surprises me. It's been this way for a long time and will probably always be. I guess this is why mama constantly tells my brother and me to always provide for our children when we have them—no matter what the circumstances are at the time!

Oh!

Let me hurry up and finish writing in my diary. It's almost 9:00 p.m. on the clock that sits on my nightstand. This particular clock shows the *correct* time of day. The clock on my dresser, next to my bucket of hair bows, is set *10 minutes ahead*. I keep that one set ahead so that I am always *'prepared'*. Prepared in the sense that I allow myself extra time when I need it. Mama and Khoi think my time-keeping methods are crazy and confusing, but I function just fine with 'em.

Either way, mama is going to be in here soon to tuck me into bed.

Giggling inside, I sometimes amuse my own self with the things I do. Especially last winter when I became so bored one day that I reset all the clocks in the house. I reset them anywhere from the correct time up to fifteen minutes ahead. I thought it was a neat idea, but, of course, mama didn't agree. She became so "throwed-off" from what I'd done till she had to rely on her own wrist watch for the 'true time' of day. She punished me behind all of this, too; stating, "She didn't know if she was coming or going dealing with such uncertainties of time".

I'm yawning uncontrollably, but I must first get these last words down in my diary. Once she gives us our *Hugs and Kisses Time*, she doesn't expect any activity to be heard or seen from within our bedrooms.

Rhyah's Diary Entry:

There's been plenty of Sundays since Children's Day. Up until now, no one, except Morgan, has even mentioned my catastrophe on that day. Kristi has a new cell phone. I want one, too, but mama refuses to get me one. I asked daddy if he would buy me one, but he most likely won't, either. He promised to call us, but still hasn't done so. 5th grade is going fine. The next Honor Roll list is coming out soon. Next year, I'll be in the 6th grade. I'll be in middle school, then, and able to switch classes. I won't have the same old, boring teacher all day long. I still feel that I am too old not to be able to ride the school bus. Mama takes us and picks us up from school every day. She doesn't take a lunch-break in order to manage it. Khoi's football team appeared in the newspaper today. They remain undefeated; the same as last year. Mama cut the article out and inserted it into the frame that holds our family portrait. Mama had us to clean out our closets. She's going to donate all of our old clothes and shoes to a charity group. Afterwards, I moved all of my warmer clothes to the front of my closet, including my favorite winter coat.

Rhyah

"Oh! No!
The closet!
The coat closet at church!!!"

"Someone's going to find that fan tray soon." I inwardly shout, slamming my diary shut.

Afterwards, I close my eyes to think about how long it's actually been since I'd hidden that tray. Well, the temperature flip-flopped three or four days ago, so, I know someone will find the tray in the near future. Afterall, it's tucked away in the church's coat closet.

Coats.

Closet.

Coats.

Closet.

They go together during this time of year. Not only have the leaves been turning gold, but they're beginning to fall off the trees, too.

'True-fall' has finally arrived; pushing the warmer weather away. Someone's going to be using that **coat closet** soon!!! . . . and by this, my secret will be brought forward.

And then, Rev. Reeves . . .

Ohhhhh!!!! Nooooo!!!!

(I don't even wanna think about it.)

He'll find out.

He'll find out some way.

I don't know how, but he will.

He always seems to find out about everything.

He'll, in turn, dedicate a bone-chilling sermon on *the once missing fans!* I can see him now—clenching his jaws before going into a stormy rampage. He would stand at that pulpit thrusting his bible in front of some *innocent person.*

And ooohhhh . . . the hollering he'll be doing.

Yelling and screaming at someone or maybe even the whole congregation . . . and all for nothing!

"I don't want *anyone else* to be falsely accused during one of his brutal sermons.

That wouldn't be right.

It wouldn't be fair, either.

Nor, do I want this to be on my own conscious forever." I sadly acknowledge from within with a heart heavy of remorse.

"How could I have forgotten about this for so long?" I quietly anguish. Lying on propped-up pillows, I begin to replay all of The Children's Day events over and over in my mind. Still, I find no peace; just an overwhelming feeling of panic.

"There must have been some point from that day till now that I could have returned the fan tray safely back into the O'Peniel's storage room without anyone catching me." I come to wonder.

I give one strong pull at my bed's comforter in *disgrace*; covering up my body and my face, too.

I am so ashamed.

Somehow, I am going to have to sneak back into that **coat closet** and put the fan tray back into the storage room; its usual and proper place.

I hear mama's footsteps heading toward my room. Her steps are tight and quick tonight; one nestled right behind the other. Instantly, I throw the comforter forward in order not to appear guilty of anything. It seems mama wears a radar-detector on her forehead to sense any forms of danger concerning Khoi or I.

"Rhyah Ann, put that diary away!" she commands.

"It's time to go to bed. Remember to say your prayers . . . and I love you," she adds.

We hug and kiss after that.

Mama attempts to leave, but instinctively seizes the doorframe to turn back around. She looks my room over and finds that my diary is sitting closed, but with its strings loose on my dresser.

With one of her tight-eyed looks, ". . . and tie its strings," she abruptly expresses.

"Whew!" I was beginning to think she'd been reading my mind or something concerning the missing fan tray.

Mama does another little stunt every so often, too. She has to make sure the diary is actually closed, its ribbons are tied, and it's obviously been put away.

I hear her footsteps stop at Khoi's bedroom door. She's probably making sure he has fallen asleep already. Or, knowing my brother—that he hasn't turned that video game system back on.

Her footsteps resume.

Eventually, they fade away as she enters into her own room.

I lay in my bed thinking, unable to doze-off. Ideas of the strange ways grown people act seem to keep consuming me. People; especially, grown-ups, act as curious as the shapes of these stars outside my bedroom window.

Particularly, here recently.

Every since I made the fan tray disappear, very bizarre behaviors have erupted concerning our church members.

Come to think of it, Mr. Le Geaux and his family stopped coming to church the third Sunday after I hid the fans. His wife sang in the choir. She certainly sang off key, but she always gave Khoi and I nice birthday gifts.

"Hmmm . . . whom else?" I wonder peering over at my diary's ribbons.

Well, I can't remember exactly whom, but there are a few more open seats among the pews. Surely more than there has been in the past. Well, way more empty seats than when Rev. Reeves took over preaching at O'Peniel.

Oh, yea! One Sunday morning, I did witness one member get out of her car, only to crack-open the double doors of the church. With her body lowered to the height of a midget, she peeked into the foyer. Then, promptly closed the door after noticing there weren't any fans laying there for her retrieval. I even watched as she raced back to her car. Hunched over the steering wheel, she consequently drove out of the parking lot and whisked out of sight. I haven't seen her at church since that morning, either.

More women have begun to wear hats to church. I guess,—well, I know—as a result of me having hidden the church fans. Aunt Jan makes sure she's always geared up every Sunday.

She's worn a different hat each Sunday since the fans vanished.

These women's hats are not for *show* because they're worn tilted; as to not allow any eye contact to be made from Rev. Reeves.

Lately, only those who happen to arrive early to church are *blessed* to receive a 'fan'. There were some fans left, though, by mistake from those who visited O'Peniel on 'Children's Day'. In addition, a handful of 'em have been made out of paper plates glued to Popsicle sticks by Bro. Carrington. He even shaped 'em to look a lot like real church fans, too.

Recently, another one of our deacons attended a church service in town just to pick up whatever extra fans he could from there.

All of these different types of *replacement fans* now sit in a collection plate as you enter the foyer. Yes, indeed. One of our church's collection plates is now the substitute for our fan tray. Those who aren't lucky enough to receive a fan—*of some sort*—have been using their church programs as simple alternatives.

Rev. Reeves never did agree to the deacon board's request to purchase any new hand fans. He responded to the board's request at the church's last business meeting. He decided that all extra money had to go directly to the church's building fund. I found this out by overhearing Grandmommy and mama talk almost a month ago. Duchesne's Funeral Home donates new fans to local churches every year around Christmas time, but that's still a ways away!

The sheep are calling me, but my mind keeps drifting back on those church fans. O'Peniel cannot move forward till I get those fans back into the storage room.

Leaving my bed to kneel by its side, I begin to pray:

RHYAH'S PRAYER:

"Dear Lord! Please, allow me to be able to get the fan
tray back into that storage room
without being noticed."
On both knees, I continue praying. But now, with my
hands pressed pointing toward Heaven.
"O' Lord Jesus, Grandmommy, mama and even Rev.
Reeves, himself, have said,
we all have sinned, so, please, forgive me!
I am asking for forgiveness
because your Father is a forgiving God.
P-L-E-A-S-E, pardon me for the sin of having hidden
the fan tray, P-L-E-A-S-E.
I just do not think people should have to live their lives
by always using *cover-ups*!
We all have skeletons in our **closets**!
*"Oh! . . . there's that word again (**closet**)! . . . and it's
beginning to make me feel terrible even more than before!"*
But, Rev. Reeves notoriously seems to make people
relive their pasts over and over again; particularly,
if it was of a dark one.
He acts like the church house is his courtroom.
The bible: his gavel.
The pulpit: his bench.
He, himself: judge *and* jury.
And the punishment: always a hard-hitting sermon of
his choosing.
Will he not be satisfied until all the members just get
up—walking out of church one day while he even
preaches a dreary sermon?
Would this finally prove a point to him?
Would then, the *'fan—affair'* end?

I know I am only a kid, but I confess from my lips to
Your ears, that I too, have done wrong.
In Jesus' name, please GOD,
please continue to guide me.
Oh, yea! Thanks to my guardian angel for continuing
to carry on our special deal.

"The truth will set you free!!" automatically enters into my mind
as I pitifully climb back into bed. I wonder now whether God just
told my guardian angel to send those words to me for comfort. I lay
in bed continuing to quietly pray that no one will catch me trying
to replace the fan tray back into its appropriate place.

CHAPTER 39

The Ordeal I

Three *long* days have passed since I first remembered the *'fan tray ordeal'*.

And I have had nothing else, but this on my mind. I don't want this to start affecting my ability to study or concentrate in school. Ooohhhweee, if this begins to interfere with my grades and I get dropped from Honor Classes, mama will have a hissy fit! I must act fast or all of this worrying will persist.

I have been continually pressuring myself about the matter: "Should I sneak back in the coat closet before church or wait until church is over in order to replace the tray of fans?

Better yet, *HOW*?

Even more importantly, at what POINT before or after church?" I again probe.

> *"Please Lord,"* I quickly start praying getting out of bed this morning. *"It's another day; another new Sunday. I could barely sleep last night. I tossed and turned in torment behind my ordeal. Please guide me, Lord. Please make a way allowing me to return the church's fans to the storage room undetected."*

"Is everyone up?" mama calmly calls out from her bedroom in a shallow voice.

There seems to be, I don't know, . . . maybe an absence of or excitement about her this morning. Mornings are usually the best times of the day for her, though.

Yesterday evening, Aunt Jan called Aunt Gayla to apparently ask if she wanted to wear one of her hats to church this morning. Together, they called mama.

From my viewpoint, it seems that the missing fans are really taking a toll on O'Peniel!

I overheard mama tell both of them, "What happens in the dark, will come to light . . . those fans didn't just walk away . . . and that she did not need to wear a hat or use anything else at church because God was her protective armor."

Their conversation went on as she informed 'em that for the last several days, she had began to feel sorta weak again. And that those missing fans weren't going to add to her condition. She also made it known that *that devil is a lie!* when Aunt Jan further inquired about mama needing to shield herself some sorta way.

Remembering their conversation last night stirs up a funny feeling in my stomach. It's a weird sensation. One that I first felt after remembering how long ago I'd put the fans in coat **closet** at church. This, along with realizing the obvious fact that it has turned much cooler outside. Church members will need to hang up their coats in that **closet.**

That word again!—*closet*!" I recall covering my face with sweaty hands,

"Oh! No!"

CHAPTER 40

The Ordeal II

Khoi and I have just finished eating cold cereal for breakfast. My nerves had removed half of my appetite, so I ate much less than him. He ate two full bowls while I ended up mainly pouring most of my one and only bowl out.

Mama has only gotten out of bed to go to the bathroom and to make sure we'd at least eaten something.

After breakfast, he and I get dressed.

The lavender hair bow draped and tied around my ponytail is just not enough to complete the look I desire. I keep looking in the mirror, but I still feel as if I am missing something this morning.

I peak into mama's bedroom to find her laying there stroking both of her legs.

The look on her face spells pain.

Pretending not to have noticed anything different about her, "Do I look o.k. for church, mama?" I question.

Mama glances at me, but does not speak. She only rises from her bed wearing her favorite flannel pajamas. Those baby blue ones sprinkled with tiny pink and yellow dots. With care, she grabs her thick robe off the edge of the bed and enters into her walk-in closet.

In there, she suggests a gift daddy once gave her. Mama kneels down while holding onto me. She stirs around a bit among some stacked items. Her fragile body trembles as she rises back up carrying a silver box in her hand.

The box has mama's name engraved on the top of it. It's also lined in red velvet.

She keeps this box buried beneath an old photo album that only contains pictures of her and my daddy. Mama then shows me a beautiful string of pearls that lay in between her fingers. She sluggishly steps behind me.

"Awe." I marvel.

She gracefully fastens them around my neck.

Between gasps, "Mama, these look brand new. Have you ever worn 'em?"

Standing behind me, "Once or twice," she whispers.

Mama gradually moves back around to face me.

For a better look, she takes a couple of steps backward and expresses, "You are growing up, Rhyah. One day, you'll be a grown woman."

She then lowers her hand to further say, "Just always do what's right and you will be successful at anything you set your little heart to."

"Maybe someday these pearls will be yours," she adds.

Afterwards, mama turns away attempting to select a dress for church.

While looking back toward her closet, I leave her bedroom so that she can get dressed. From outside her bedroom, all I can see is mama's shadow sticking out of her closet.

It's a frail silhouette that moves about very slowly.

Nevertheless, I'm sure she'll be o.k, reassuring myself drifting back up the hallway.

"But, what if something did happen to her?"

My head drops with the simple thought of not having mama around.

"Who would take care of us?

Grandmommy?" I instantly acknowledge walking slowly and watching the lines on our wooden floor.

"Would Khoi and I still have our own rooms?

What would be of us?

As for daddy?

Would he then be there for us?"

Mama always seems to stay on top of everything. Or, at least that's the way I see it.

Neither Khoi nor I currently have any needs. Plenty of wants maybe, but never any needs. Would our lives still be the same if she weren't around? What if she did really die someday as a consequence of her blood disease? Or, from anything else as far as that's concerned?

Would Rev. Reeves have to eulogize her?

"Oh, my goodness!

I hope not!

That wouldn't be proper enough for mama.

All he'd do is scream over her casket and probably swat at it with his bible.

As I get closer to the TV room, I heard a sports announcer blatantly broadcast, "Will today's game make or break this number 1 team?" through our surround sound speakers that Daddy installed.

Still concerned about mama, I sit down next to Khoi who's waiting on Uncle Sherman to arrive.

Khoi scurries for the remote control.

"Click, click."

He flips along the stations. He sits here watching various highlights of some 'big-time' football game that's to be held today.

Drawn only to sports channels, he clicks a few more times.

"Today is the big game-breaker of this division!" a different sports announcer tells the world.

I begin to reflect on the beautiful strand of pearls around my neck and the unique box mama keeps 'em in. She keeps other memories in this box, as well. Khoi's locks from his first haircut are in there. All of our baby teeth are in there. A dried up ol' red rose that's been sealed in plastic is kept in there, too. No telling what else she cherishes enough to keep in that box. Papa Joseph bought mama a high school graduation gift that came in that silver box. It holds valuable memories and she's kept it ever since.

Thinking of boxes and gifts, "Khoi, by the way, what did daddy get you for your birthday? You didn't open your gift at the party and I've been forgetting to ask you what you'd received from him."

He only shrugs a shoulder.

"You don't remember?"

He shrugs his shoulder for a second time, but only harder this time; as if to say *I'm getting on his nerves.*

". . . Or, do you mean you have not opened it yet?"

Without saying a word, he exhales noisily and jumps up; moving closer to the other end of the sofa.

We become statues sitting here watching television.

Out of the corner of my eye, I notice Khoi tugging at his church shirt in preparation to chew on it . . . getting it ready for what is going to be a 'tug-o-war' between him versus the shirt. I'm not too sure, but I also believe I overheard him mumble something about daddy, then, mention Uncle Sherman's name in a softer voice.

CHAPTER 41

The Ordeal III

Mama is still kinda moving slowly. I hear her shuffling up the hallway in her house shoes.

A mellow "awww" . . ." echoes softly from within the hallway, too.

As she shifts closer, I can't help but notice that her dress is leaning off her left shoulder. It must not be zipped up all the way, either. I see its tag sticking straight-up in the back.

Plus, her hair has not yet been brushed.

Bit by bit, mama makes it into the dining room. Subsequently, she sits down in a dining room chair; unable to make it to the kitchen. Usually, her first order of business each morning is to take one of those horse-looking pills.

I can only figure, she certainly must be sick since that room is only used for holidays or special occasions.

Her next move—to simply lay her head onto the table.

Her long hair rests there, too.

I rush toward her!

"Mama, what's wrong?" *"Are the moons in your body hurting you real bad right now?"* I probe in a panic.

She isn't answering.

Nor, is she looking at me.

Pulling back her stretched-out hair, I begin to finish zipping up her dress, but *stop* right away when I hear her struggling deeply for air.

Pointing to the telephone with one hand, mama directs, "Call an ambulance and Dr. Burton's paging service". Obviously in great pain, she continues to clutch at her chest with her other hand.

Dr. Burton's telephone number is written on a piece of paper that's taped to the bottom of the telephone in our TV room.

Grandmommy placed it under there when Khoi and I were younger.

I called 911 first, like mama told me to and then Dr. Burton.

Khoi picks up on what's going on in our dining room and comes to help mama onto the TV room's sofa.

Immediately afterwards, I call Grandmommy.

Grandmommy reaches our house about thirty seconds before the ambulance does. Probably, because she drove over here lightning-fast with her hazard lights on.

I can hear sirens becoming louder and clearer as the ambulance travels down our street. Plus, Khoi, who's crying uncontrollably, leaves our front door open as he runs outside to meet Grandmommy. In the beginning, the sirens sounded like far-away whistles. But, now they sound just like they always do at the end of The Black History Parade; loud enough to puncture your eardrums. Aunt Gayla arrives shortly after the paramedics do—frantic and running toward the house in her own classy-kinda way.

Uncle Sherman finally arrives to pick up Khoi, too. He pulls up only moments later than Aunt Gayla. Surprised to find an ambulance backed into our driveway, he sprints toward the front door.

The paramedics begin to work on mama immediately.

The two of 'em work together at inserting a skinny-looking plastic needle into her arm and place an oxygen mask over her face. The needle has a long tube attached to it that one paramedic wraps around his shoulder.

The other paramedic guardedly feels mama's hands and legs before calling out some information to the other one who's holding mama's long tube. They're using words I have never heard before. Grandmommy offers 'em some added information pertaining to mama's circumstances. She even carefully removes mama's socks to point to her ankles and toe nails. Subsequently, more notes are taken.

Eventually, a blanket is ripped from its packaging and is loosely placed over most of her body.

"Step back a little kids. Try not to touch her. She's o.k." The male paramedic advises my brother and I.

Mama still has not said too much up to this point. Her crumpled eyelids and moans speak for it all, though. In so much pain, a tear escapes each eye every time she squeezes them shut.

Letting out louder moans, Grandmommy kisses the portion of the blanket covering mama's chest area. Feeling that a kiss will be sufficient, Grandmommy knows not to actually touch mama, either. For some reason, people going through a crisis cannot bear being touched.

The pain, as intense as it must be, causes mama to let out one more moan that turns into a low scream.

Khoi, in anguish and crying real, real hard, jumps up and down without his feet ever leaving the floor.

Ignoring him, "Relax, ma'am. Your pain meds. have now been administered.

Let them begin to work," the male paramedic begins telling her. Mama removes her hand from her chest and tries to grab at one of her legs.

"Relax, o.k. In about 10 more seconds, you'll start to feel much, much better." The female paramedic compassionately tells mama.

Mama's clasped mouth doesn't allow her to respond. She just continues to hold her chest with her 'free arm'—the arm without the needle in it.

The paramedics are preparing her for the ride to the hospital as they pack a lot of equipment back into a large, green box with handles.

Out of the blue, the female paramedic asks, "Who made the call to 911 for her? We received notice that it was from a young child."

Unaware of her reason for wanting to know, I raise my hand, like I do in school.

She praises me for my actions and reassures Khoi and I that mama is going to be fine. "You're brave and you're smart. You sure handled yourself well while communicating with the dispatcher earlier," the other paramedic tells me.

Grandmommy starts patting my back once this is all said.

"Hmmm. I've never seen a female paramedic before.

She's nice.

Well, really both she and the male paramedics are polite and helpful," are my thoughts observing how swiftly they are able to lift her stretcher.

Even though I want to (and it's killing me not to), I knew better than to begin asking questions at a time like this. I have so many questions rising in my mind right now till it could burst open. How do I put it . . . well, you know when you begin blowing up a balloon and it gets bigger and bigger—and then it bursts. A swollen feeling is another way to explain it.

As mama is carried down our sidewalk to the ambulance, Khoi runs after her.

After all, it's been a while since we've seen her in such a 'low state'.

I remember Aunt Gayla having to remain at our house the last time mama was rushed to the hospital. We were much younger then, though.

Khoi's still crying non-stop and is tightly gripping mama's 'free hand'.

Uncle Sherman learns he's partially blocking the ambulance, so, he leaves to go on to church. Before he drives off, he asks Aunt Gayla to text him about mama's status on his cell phone.

Khoi continues to clutch mama's 'free hand' that's obviously turning paler. He won't permit the paramedics to place her into the awaiting ambulance. He refuses to let her hand go. So, Aunt Gayla takes his hand and replaces mama's with her own hand.

Grandmommy, by now, has locked our front door and is already waiting in her car. Her car's flashing yellow lights are on again. Aunt Gayla coaxes Khoi and me to quickly get into her car. We travel to the hospital closely behind Grandmommy, who's not leaving too much space between she and the ambulance.

Aunt Gayla, "I have *a funny feeling* in my stomach right now." I break to tell her while firmly clutching onto mama's pearls.

"Sweetie, your mom is going to be just fine. Remember what the paramedic just said back at the house," she swiftly tells me.

"No!

No ma'am, Auntie Gayla!

Not about mama . . . I mean . . . I mean . . . A different kinda funny feeling.

One that makes you feel really strange when you think about something.

Ya' know, one that keeps you up at night."

Aunt Gayla is trying to focus on driving. She seems to want to answer me, but only stutters over her first couple of words. Structured as she is, she can barely concentrate on my questions on top of following Grandmommy.

Risking a lecture, I try again at getting her to understand me.

"Is this the funny feeling people sometimes get and label it a *'wake-up call?'*" I question seeking a direct answer. "It very well may be," She replies tightly holding the wheel. "Usually when a person gets that kind of feeling, he or she will try to make a change in their lives for the better.

It's also another way of saying your *'conscious is speaking to you'* about something. Putting it simply, Rhyah, people must *'make a wrong; right'* in order to feel better in regretful situations. But, when God puts His hand in the situation, everything will always move perfectly," she responds while keeping a close eye on Grandmommy—and the ambulance, too.

"Why do you ask?"

"Huh? . . . ohhh, no specific reason, I guess." I reply.

At this point, I knew my guardian angel had to be near. It had clearly spoken to me once more, . . . and without a doubt, through Aunt Gayla, too.

First, *it* did when I was saying my prayers the other night. And now here in the car . . . and I must not forget this morning when mama advised me to always do what is right.

"I have to do what is right! I have done wrong and I have to correct the problem!"

CHAPTER 42

The Parking Garage

The front of Khoi's shirt is really wet, now. His cheeks appear soggier than a mushy sponge.

. . . . And swollen full.

. . . . And really red.

He sheds quiet tears all the way to the hospital. We can barely understand him trying to talk. All we can assume is that he is trying to give us his version as to how mama looked once the paramedics began to start attaching those 'things' to her.

We arrive at St. Mary's Catholic Hospital. It's the only hospital in town. It's a tall, red-bricked hospital and it's also where my brother and I were born. Besides St. Mary's, there are only 3 other smaller hospitals within this whole parish.

After turning two sharp corners, we reach the parking garage's entrance.

Aunt Gayla snatches a ticket stub from an automatic dispenser. Quickly moving forward, she almost bumps into its (mechanical) entrance lever.

Level one; full.

We reach level two; it's also full.

Levels three and four; same story.

As it is, each time Aunt Gayla 'guns-it' to the next level, (barely missing other parked cars); we consistently see blinking signs that read: 'This Parking Level Filled'.

Turns out, there are no empty parking spaces on its first four levels.

So, finally she has to park on the 5th level; the very top floor of the parking garage.

By surprise, the garage's elevator isn't working, either.

Therefore, we have to walk down all 5 flights of stairs.

Well, this, for sure, upsets Aunt Gayla—to say the least!—And she's wearing high heels, too! Boiling mad, she keeps a tight grip onto Khoi's left shoulder as we begin our third flight down.

Feeling her discomfort, "Aunt Gayla, why don't you just take your heels off?

And then, you might not be in as much pain."

". . . . and have to walk on these dirty, bare steps . . . and these damp floors . . . Oh, my Lord, Rhyah! Are you serious?" Her voice loudly echoes throughout the stairwell.

"No telling *what or who's* been in here!" she continues her fuss while trying to keep a sense of balance. By now, Khoi is walking all hunched over—hobbling toward each step with Aunt Gayla's weight in-tow. (All from her now pressing down real hard on his whole back.) Khoi makes sure to keep her steady. It appears that he's truly trying to help stabilize her. He'd better. Because, if he knew like I knew: for sure, Aunt Gayla would never let him live it down if she accidentally slipped and fell or something.

She's just about out of breath as we reach the bottom floor of the stairwell. Out of breath, her loud breathing seems to be bouncing off these concrete walls.

Full of anger, she makes Khoi and I walk all the way around to the front of the parking garage so that she can complain to the ticket agent about their elevator problem.

The woman in the booth tries to explain to Aunt Gayla that any problems associated with the elevator are not her responsibility. But, Aunt Gayla, pushy and persistent as ever, won't hear of it!

Still out of breath, "This is t-o-t-a-l-l-y unacceptable!" she continues on with loudly.

With hell in her face, she then points to her aching feet. Both arms fly up as she cries out, "Later, I will pay good money to have parked in this garage and the accommodations are horrible! . . .

And did you know that we had to park on level five because your garage is practically full!

Plus, level five is an uncovered area . . .

And might I further inform you that I drive a very expensive car—one that sits atop your garage—able to be exposed to the elements.

THIS i-s u-t-t-e-r-l-y r-i-d-i-c-u-l-o-u-s!"

"Ma'am, AGAIN, I am not the one to complain to. You can call the telephone number on the back of your parking ticket if you'd like to. Furthermore, the elevator problem was reported to a maintenance technician this morning, O.K.!" The woman snap s back.

The ticket agent is still only making excuses as Auntie Gayla sees it.

She keeps arguing until the lady has to slam the ticket window shut in her face!

Embarrassed, Khoi and I have already begun to walk toward the hospital as if we weren't even with her.

Angrier than a bull seeing red, Aunt Gayla still doesn't care.

She, nonetheless, continues going off on that lady through the closed window.

She even ignores the other cars beginning to line-up waiting to pay and exit. She's attracting the attention of all of the people walking near her; with some even stopping to stare.

With no doubt, I know she's surely letting that ticket agent have it by now!

The lady may not be able to hear Aunt Gayla too well through that closed window, but she can surely read her body language.

With my aunt's neck rolling around; no doubt, that agent clearly knows how my aunt feels by now.

Still embarrassed by her actions, Khoi and I keep on moving toward the emergency room's entrance.

Noticing that we're leaving her behind, Aunt Gayla eventually catches up with us.

I can hear her now walking hard in those heels behind us; grumbling between each deep breath.

CHAPTER 43

Small Talk and Enormous Beliefs

"Hey! There's Grandmommy's car!" Khoi abruptly yells out. With a body that's still slightly hung forward, he attempts to jet off toward it.

"No! Wait, honey. This way," Aunt Gayla says catching his shirt collar. "Grandmommy's inside the hospital. She's already in there with your mom," she impatiently concludes.

Grandmommy apparently wasted no-time trying to find a parking space. She's parked in a section near the emergency room's entrance. But, it's in an area clearly marked for ambulances and disabled people. Blue and white wheelchair signs are posted in front of all of this section's parking spots. There's even faded blue and white signs painted on the ground notifying people who unlawfully attempt to park there.

We arrive inside mama's holding room and see that Dr. Burton's made it here, too.

He probably arrived before Grandmommy. This is the room a patient is held in before being released to a regular room.

Dr. Burton's been treating her for this disorder since she was about my age.

He's discussing mama's current status with Grandmommy.

Using his thesascope to point at mama, "At this point, the oxygen level in her blood stream is very, very low. Plus, I've already placed an order for her to undergo the chest x-rays to determine if there are any deficiencies," he tells Grandmommy.

Mama is listening at them, but with heavy eyes.

By looking at mama, I, too, can tell something is way wrong.

Her eyes and fingernails have turned that yellowy-brownish color.

Her pale skin is puffy around the wrists and ankles. I listen-in as he mentions that mama also feels faint and is extremely fatigued. Khoi and I focus on him reporting that in critical cases such as this one, mama's blood is subject to become infected or even poisoned . . . just because her oxygen level has gotten so low.

Dr. Burton looks at mama and then uses his pen to firmly tap on her chart before saying, "The reason why? . . . Is because you always wait too long before coming to my office or before coming to this emergency room. When you begin to feel weak, you ought to know by now, that I want you to either come see me immediately or to come here! A crisis can come on without any warning, Vanessa. You know that."

Mama acknowledges him by barely shaking her head.

Well, no one can hear mama reply anyway because of the oxygen mask she's wearing.

Aunt Gayla whispers to Grandmommy that she's about to step out to go and leave Uncle Sherman a voice-mail message. Remembering that Uncle Sherman had said to text him, not call him, I wanted to remind Aunt Gayla, but I chose not to out of fear that she might still be angry over the parking issue.

Dr. Burton notices my brother and me staring at mama. He explains to us, as mama has done in the past that Sickle Cell Disease causes the majority of her red blood cells to form into tiny sickled ones. In order to give us a better description, he begins to draw awkward looking figures on her hospital chart. After that, he tells us that these funny shaped cells jam up mama's blood vessels. When this process begins, the pain does, too.

My brother really isn't focusing anymore on what Dr. Burton is saying, but I am.

I take mental notes and try to make sense of his drawings.

The shapes he's sketched do look similar to the ones mama's described in the past.

Mama has told us that Khoi, daddy and I have something called a 'trait'. I really don't understand it all too clearly. I just know that I won't ever really get sick like she does.

Mama has a tall, silver rack with big hooks positioned next to her hospital bed.

The silver rack looks to be a little smaller than my daddy.

Listening on, Dr. Burton tells Grandmommy that the 3 clear bags connected to the rack contain an antibiotic medication, another fluid that I cannot remember the name of, and finally, a medicine bag for pain.

I do remember him telling her that mama's medicine for pain begins with the letter 'm' and has an 'f' sound in the middle of its name. This pain medication has a pump linked to the rack. It's a pump that mama can push at any time on her own.

She pushed it a minute ago before adjusting its long cord.

After doing so, she changed positions in bed. She also has a total of 3 long and skinny tubes taped to both arms. Before leaving home, the paramedics had only one tube attached to one of her arms. Now she has three; one in one arm and two in the other.

Mama pushes the tall rack further backward in order to distract Khoi and me from standing here staring at it.

She attempts to speak, but rather chooses to actively motion for us to come toward her. Mama hugs us. She seems to do so with all her might.

After we three hug, she balls her body up.

Aunt Gayla returns to mama's room.

Shortly thereafter, Dr. Burton leaves allowing for more space in the room.

Aunt Gayla takes our hands and guides Khoi and myself to a pair of seats near mama's bed. Mama lays there quiet and undisturbed.

Grandmommy makes sure to catch a passing nurse. Pointing toward mama, "Could she get an extra warm blanket and a pair of socks, please?" "Sure, but it may take a moment since I'll have to make those requests from two separate departments." the nurse tells her.

Aunt Gayla exits our room again. But this time, in search of a pay phone.

Before leaving, she explains to Grandmommy that she's having problems trying to contact my Uncle Sherman. The way she kept hitting buttons, I could tell that she was having problems getting a good reception from her cell phone within this area of the hospital.

A wave of silence overcomes the room. Trying to lighten the mood, Grandmommy initiates some 'small talk' between Khoi and I. 'Small talk' or perhaps 'stuff' just to distract us.

Stuff like: what do we want for Christmas? Or, when was the last time we visited our town's library? The conversation mainly consists of she and I because Khoi never enters into any of the discussions.

The nurse still has not brought back mama's extra blanket or socks, so Grandmommy goes in search of the items. Before leaving, she pulls back the long, white curtains that cover a big window next to mama's bed.

First, grandmommy rips back the left side of the curtain.

Then, the right to give off plenty of sunlight in here.

The sunlight pierces through the window aiming straight toward mama's cradled body. Its light glows so bright that it appears to have the same energy as that crystal angel hanging up at O'Peniel. Enough energy that my brother and I just sit here being mesmerized by it; something like being held in a trance.

These curtains also remind me of the ones in Grandmommy's house, only thicker—with a hem that appears to be the length of a shoe.

Aunt Gayla guardedly re-approaches mama's room.

She uses her keys to lightly tap on the room's door.

After that, she sticks her head inside, then, pushes the ajar door open even further.

Quickly twisting her arm to glance at her wrist watch, "Come on guys, let's go," she quietly states. "I can tell we're already going to be late for church. Grandmommy is going to stay here with your mom." I had already figured that, though. Grandmommy has a deep bond with all of her children.

Aunt Gayla turns away from mama's room thinking we're following her into the hospital's hallway. She meets up with Grandmommy whose at the nurse's station waiting on the items she requested for mama.

Through the slightly cracked door, I see Grandmommy carrying a whole bundle of blankets, not just the single blanket she'd previously requested.

No socks, though.

Mama always wears socks.

Even in the height of summer.

Grandmommy's holding the blankets close to her heart; as close as she does her bible during prayer times at church.

I overhear Grandmommy repeating to Aunt Gayla of the exact location as to where she's illegally parked. They need to switch cars for some reason.

"Gayla Marie, take my car since yours is at least parked legally. Here are my keys."

In exchange, Aunt Gayla gives Grandmommy her sets of keys and her ticket stub. At that moment, I hear Aunt Gayla start-in again on the confrontation she previously had with the ticket agent—speaking with that same body posture.

Despite Aunt Gayla's previous request for us to have followed her, Khoi and I remain in mama's room.

"I wish mama felt better." I lowly remark to Khoi.

He doesn't answer.

Mama, asleep now, is really looking feeble.

Khoi is no longer staring at the light, but at mama, as I am.

She lays there so motionless, but, more so, at ease.

Her stronger pain medication has definately kicked-in.

Mama reminds me of the lady in the bible who had had *problems with her own blood for 12 years.* Jesus healed this lady because she had *enormous faith* as she touched the hem of His garment.

"Maybe this sorta *thing* can work for mama, too," I'm imagining.

Hurriedly, I step past Khoi and head toward the window.

I cross through the brilliant sunlight to grab the right side of the curtain.

I pull it forward—toward mama's bed; as far as it can go in order to reach her hands.

I allow its hem to *touch* her hands and (in my mind) I ask Jesus to ask God to do for mama what He did for that lady in the bible.

Khoi's damp shirt immediately drops from his mouth.

"Whatcha doing?" he asks, focusing first on the curtain and then on me.

I remind him of the sick lady in the bible who was healed while pointing directly at the curtain's hem.

Aunt Gayla, peeking in at us, clears her throat.

Knowing my Aunt Gayla, this means to come on right now!

I instantly get up and head toward the door, but not forgetting the hem and my prayer to God.

Khoi starts to get up, too, but instead of following me, he turns back around and grabs the same portion of the hem I'd had.

He moves about carelessly with the curtain; bumping into mama's silver, medicine rack and the night stand.

"Boing!"

His right foot accidentally kicks a wheel under her bed. Mama's eyelids flutter for a moment, but never really open.

And if that's not enough, the right side of his body then hits a part of mama's bed; shaking it slightly.

She begins to reposition herself, but never wakes up.

This does not stop Khoi, at all! He quickly places the same hemmed portion I'd had back into mama's hands. He squeezes her fingers securely around it.

Sleeping deeply, mama does not even seem to notice.

We carefully close the door behind us. Tears are dribbling down Khoi's cheeks again. Instead of using the front of his shirt, he raises both arms to use his sleeves at wiping 'em away. The front of his shirt was already noticeably wet. Now, his sleeves are, too.

Grandmommy and Aunt Gayla are standing right outside mama's room.

They, along with a nurse, are discussing how long mama will probably be hospitalized. That, along with the fact that her socks hadn't arrived.

Aunt Gayla sees Khoi and me walking toward 'em and impatiently looks at us.

She grumbles some words in a sense that only mama could use when we've gotten on her nerves in public. Grandmommy uses her own fingers to wipe away Khoi's excess tears before hugging us good-bye.

I felt the warmth of the blankets between her and me during our hug.

Aunt Gayla straightens Khoi's collar and firmly tucks in the back of his shirt before we start down a hallway that leads to Grandmommy's car.

Auntie Gayla and Khoi lead the way.

Then myself; holding up the rear.

Making our way out, I notice the same bright light that was beaming into mama's room. It's now following us through the large plated windows in this hallway. Seeing these beaming rays lets me know that this is *God's **sign*** alerting me that He's gotten Khoi and my messages pertaining to mama.

"Thank you, God," I whisper to myself.

CHAPTER 44

A Twisted Stomach

We get to church after the announcements have been read.

The choir has already sung . . . *and thank God for that!*

I see that the collection plate has already reached the far end of church meaning that it has already passed the section we normally sit in.

Uncle Sherman motions for Khoi. Probably to come over and update him on mama's status.

He uses a church program that's been folded three times to get Khoi's attention.

Finally, I review today's program.

It reads: "Keeping A Clean Folder For The Lord."

Through a windowpane, I glance at the marquee.' It reads the same, but in all capital letters.

At this point, *the funny feeling* returns.

Slight confusion, too.

"Is there still some sorta connection with this?" I ask myself reflecting on Aunt Gayla's words while on the way to the hospital along with mama's advice from earlier this morning.

I can't help but to try to overcome this feeling that keeps thrashing about inside of me.

"But, how?" I ask in doubt.

Kristi and Morgan temporarily grab my attention away from my mind-boggling thoughts.

Being messy as always, their wanting me to notice their new shoes. Morgan's are brown with wedged heels.

I can tell that Kristi's are black with smaller heels, but with strings that tie around her ankles. Kristi keeps looking at me before propping up each foot; faking as if to adjust their strings. I've seen Kristi's shoes in the mall a few weeks ago, but mama wouldn't even allow me try them on. She said that they looked too 'grown-up' for a person my age!

After that, Morgan twists her fingers through her hair.

She pulls on each curl and then allows it to spring back into place.

She pretends to only be playing with it. But in reality, she's showing me how long and bouncy her hair really is. In revenge, I gracefully roll my fingers over each pearl that droops around my neck; hoping they notice 'em, too.

Rev. Reeves takes to the pulpit carrying a *brand new bible*.

"THIS is sure to cause some gossip among the members!" I hold under my breath.

Unlike the previous one, this one's all white with black lettering on its cover.

He carries it up to the pulpit tucked underneath an armpit as if to be protecting it.

He begins today's sermon with, "Judgment day will come! Are you prepared?"

The funny feeling begins to stir-up my insides . . . working harder and harder on me . . . and sending my stomach into knots.

"Release your burdens and give them to the Lord!" Rev. Reeves hammers toward the congregation.

Thoughts of mama lying in that hospital bed seem to escape my mind.

I don't know who will be in his spotlight today, but for some unknown reason, I feel it should be me. About all I can do now is visualize the coat closet and what lay covered up inside of it.

"What I did months ago was not right.

Oh!—and how terrible I feel about it, too," lowering my chin in anguish. I go to hold-up my hanging head and see that the crystal angel is looking directly at me.

It's staring at me from within the foyer.

Predictably, Rev. Reeves pauses during his sermon.

He appears to be looking at everyone in the church through an invisible telescope . . . and for some reason, with great insight.

With steady and broad eyes, he inspects us. He reaches into his front pocket and retrieves that handkerchief.

This leads to him dabbing the sweat away from his facial area.

His nose and other parts, first.

Followed up by long rubs of the forehead and neck.

My heart begins to beat non-stop.

But, ceases when he strikes the top of the pulpit . . . not using his new bible; just both open palms of his ebony hands.

I jump!

Plenty of people around Aunt Gayla and I do, too.

Rev. Reeves then screams, "Don't let judgment day catch you with your folder incomplete or in disarray!"

'*Disarray*'??? I question as I visualize opening up my dictionary.

I don't know what '*disarray*' means, but I figure it must be something pretty bad.

Intrigued about this word, but not wanting to annoy Aunt Gayla, I try not to shuffle too much in my seat. Or, to inquire about the word's meaning.

I turn swiftly to look again at the crystal angel; only this time to find it swinging in slow motion . . . but still, appearing to be watching me.

Continuing on in his loud voice, "God is a forgiving God and He does not hold any grudges!"

"Repent! Repent this hour so that God can assign you a brand new folder!

Make it right in your life! Make it right today!" Rev. Reeves thunders.

For a moment, I *struggle* with the thought of exposing my wrongdoing before one and all:

"Will Rev. Reeves chastise me in front of the whole congregation?

Will mama punish me eternally for having caused such a commotion within the church? And Grandmommy . . . What will she think of me?

I am pretty sure Aunt Gayla will be highly disappointed in me.

Better yet, how will Uncle Sherman's step-kids react? . . . By teasing me? Of course, I answer for myself."

I don't know what to do, but it seems like Rev. Reeves has been speaking to me since he began to preaching.

Instantly, the funny feeling returns sending another wave of knots throughout my stomach. With this, my heart begins to race all over again.

I grab my churning stomach and fall back into the pew.

Determined to overcome this struggle, "I—have—got—to—act—NOW!" I shout inside.

CHAPTER 45

'Coming Face to Face With God'

While the Holy Spirit is moving Aunt Gayla, I budge from my seat and make my way toward the back of the church.

No one seems to be distracted by me leaving the sanctuary. Instead, they are focusing on all of the shouting coming from the pulpit.

Swiftly looking toward the pews, Aunt Gayla, doesn't even know I've left my seat yet.

When she does, she'll think I've just gone to the bathroom, as usual.

Still trying not to attract any attention, I take one last glimpse back at the crystal angel. Surprisingly, it gives the impression to be facing Rev. Reeves this time.

I keep walking at a speedy pace; only focusing on the rear doors ahead of me.

"Did my guardian angel, a moment ago, speak to me yet again? . . . But, through O'Peniel's crystal angel that time?

Does this mean that I, myself, have *'come face to face with God'* as well?"

Was Rev. Reeves' guardian angel trying to speak to him, too, through the crystal angel?

Did God send both of our guardian angels to help us in some way today?"

After all, the eyes of O'Peniel's crystal angel did seem to gleam at both of us a minute ago.

I pass the church's kitchen.

I know what I saw. For sure I wasn't imagining things. I wasn't and I am sure of that!

"I saw that crystal angel staring at both of us. I know I did!" I whisper reassuring myself.

Questions about it all persist in my mind as I turn down another hallway in order to reach my destination.

"That's right!" I speak out loud in realization.

"God does speak to us directly. He does so without any hesitation or deviations."

So, that must mean here lately He's been trying to get my attention in one way or another!

I've figured it out!

My guardian angel has spoken to me through others. That, and in the course of observing the crystal angel—to get His messages across.

Now I'm convinced!!!

"God, I just want to do what is right; *Your perfect will, as for me!*"

I rehearse these words over and over in my mind heading toward the coat closet. Completely focused, I soon pass a diamond-shaped, stained-glass window.

All of a sudden, a beam of bright light distracts me by striking the right side of my face.

Startled, I slow down to look around. No one's in the area as far as I can tell.

And surely no one was in the kitchen, either, when I passed it.

Once again, I steadily resume my way in the direction of the coat closet.

Without notice, the light reappears through the next stained-glass window as I pass it.

For an instant, it reminds me of the same sunlight that was in mama's hospital room and in the hospital's hallway.

"Where is this light coming from? I ask myself trying to make some sense of this issue.

In the middle of all the stained glass windows that stretch along this hallway, there's a clear, circular section.

Oddly enough, I'd never really paid too much attention to these stained glass windows before.

Amazed at how strong the lights' rays are, I ease onward toward the next window. Using the balls of my feet and my fingertips, I raise myself up to the ledge.

This time, I look directly into the circular spot. At that moment, the light seems to cover my face; blinding me momentarily.

"Could this be the same strong light from the hospital? I question again.

Amazed and unsure, I lower my body.

But, still wondering how a light could shine so brightly through a hole that size.

With clenched fists, I dab at my eyes in order to clear away the lingering glare.

Moving forward, I happen to slow down before reaching the final window in this hallway.

I gradually turn my head to face it—expecting another stream of light.

But instead; no light and no glare this time.

In its place, an image of the old man from Harry's Donut Shoppe appears in my mind.

I stand here stunned.

It was only for a split-second, but his figure was so clear that he could have really been standing right before me. "Oh! Yea! 'Slow down,'" he did happen to tell me. Then, I wouldn't miss a step. Or, was it that I wouldn't miss out on any blessings?"

Either way, I am going to take my time.

Thank you, God, for Your 'well-timed notices'.

I know my guardian angel has to be near, so God, I thank him or her, too.

Hmm . . . Did God send my guardian angel to shine those lights in my face? And if so, was that confirmation of another sign or signal?

Feeling safe, I turn around to get another glimpse of that last window.

At peace, I realize I'm *definitely on course.*

"Please God," I quickly let in, "Continue to guide me in order to carry out Your *'perfect will'* as for me."

I approach the coat closet's door with great ease.

Cautiously, I twist open its shaky knob; not wanting to disturb the dust.

First, I push aside the old choir robes that hang in here.

Then, I begin to reach down near the rear of the coat closet.

I gently raise the crumpled, choir robe to find the tray of fans sitting there just as I'd left it.

Down on my knees, I lift the tray. But, not before I clear away cobwebs and any obvious dust that has settled on it.

Only the light from the hallway assists me while I'm in here. There's no light switch in the coat closet. Probably, because it's smaller than the storage room. I rise up and close the door with as much caution as I did when I opened it.

The funny feeling inside of me seems to be mellowing a bit.

In the back of my mind, I know I am doing *'the right thing'* to overcome this awful sensation that I've been struggling with.

CHAPTER 46

A Cause to Repent

I begin carrying the fans back in the direction of the sanctuary.

Mindful of the stained glass windows, I slowly glide past 'em.

But, out the corner of my eye, I see that there's no activity. Strange as it may seem this time, there's no sudden gleam of lights from either of the windows.

Keeping focused while carrying the fan tray, I am careful as I gently push open the rear doors to the sanctuary.

Rev. Reeves, nor anyone else is aware of me re-entering. He's about to end his sermon because I see Sis. Bradley flipping through her hymn book.

"WoW!

This is a first!" I say to myself attempting to close the doors undetected.

By now, Sis. Bradley is usually already playing softly at the organ. Being that Rev. Reeves is long-winded, she starts playing when she can't take his long-winded sermons anymore. It's a hint to Rev. Reeves to start shutting *it* down. If he continues to preach, she'll begin to play harder notes that get even louder until he steps away from the pulpit altogether. But, at the moment, she remains seated flipping through her hymnal.

Rev. Reeves is the first to notice me walking toward the front of the church.

Walking between the two sections of pews, I remain guided by *His spirit*.

Using one hand, Rev. Reeves slowly adjusts his glasses as I move closer to him.

He even stops preaching for a moment. His eyes adjust briefly. He takes a look at the fan tray that hangs in my hand. A 'deer in headlights' is how he appears right now.

He firmly grasps his new bible as he makes unsuccessful attempts to carry on preaching. "The Lord . . .", ". . . . is sinning and . . .", ". . . . your folder . . ." is about all I can currently comprehend from him.

Based upon Rev. Reeves' *reaction* of seeing me, O'Peniel's entire congregation seems to position themselves for one of his outrageous outbursts.

The congregation is still unaware of my journey forward.

Replacement fans become raised: like shields.

Bodies stiffen: for modes of defense.

You'd think the man was about to throw stones at 'em.

Rev. Reeves continues to look at me.

He sucks in air. Then, quickly releases it. He seems lost for words.

With a *cause* of my own, I continue to move-in closer.

Immediately, I begin to hear ruffled words surface throughout the church.

All of O'Peniel has now taken note of me and my expedition.

My eyes begin to roam; detecting all curious reactions.

Sis. Bradley, nosey as she is, continues to hesitate before proceeding on—toward the organ. Aunt Jan raises the floppy brim of her hat to get a better view at what I'm carrying. Morgan elbows Kristi before whispering in her ear. Mrs. Carrington looks on in confusion at Bro. Carrington. He, then, stands up at attention—like one of Ms. Carolyn's guard dogs.

Rev. Reeves is still unsuccessfully trying to go on with his sermon especially since I'm the one now grabbing the congregation's attention.

Humble in spirit, I press forward, taking my time as the ol' man had instructed—carrying the fan tray and my pride both low enough to touch the floor.

With church members focusing on me, it's hard to keep my eyes fixed on one particular spot. Or, to decide as to where to lay down the fan tray.

As I become closer to the pulpit, there's no sound in the church. No movement, either.

Again, that *'holy hush'* has lay in.

(*All in all*); Aunt Gayla's 'words' in the car;
Mama's 'words' to always do what's right;
the 'bright light' in the hospital;
the 'image' of the old man in the hallway;
and thoughts of my 'guardian angel' pulsates throughout my *spiritual mind.*

Thinking about all of these events again begins to bring back that 'funny feeling' that forms knots in my stomach.

Remarkably, a loose breeze causes the crystal angel to turn slightly on its hook. Consequently, it appears to be staring at the whole congregation this time.

I feel everyone looking at my humbly bowed head and the *'unexplained'* recovery of the fan tray.

It's kinda like having eyeballs planted all around my head.

I feel as if I'm moving in slow motion.

I even sense Bro. Campbell, *'blindly'* staring at me. I'm confident he's awake right now. He certainly can't be asleep because his head follows my every move. Nor, is it bobbing up and down, as it usually does.

This middle aisle finally carries me right in front of the pulpit.

And before it—I stand here feeling shielded and protected.

Rev. Reeves' eyeglasses seem to have become a pair of binoculars. No longer a telescope.

Khoi rises up to stand on his tip toes. He lifts his chin to take a peak over Aunt Jan's hat. His shirt drops from his mouth once he sees me place the fans down before the pulpit.

In front of Rev. Reeves, his wobbly pulpit, and O'Peniel's worshippers, I place the fan tray down with little effort, but with great determination.

With her eyes bonded to me like glue, Sis. Bradley (not watching where she's going)

mistakenly approaches one of the gas heaters instead of the organ, nearly burning herself.

As I make my way back to my seat, ***"Bring your burdens to the alter . . ."*** is spoken by Rev. Reeves.

"How shocking," I express in silence.

Having heard him say this lifts my pride and reassures me that the angels in Heaven do constantly rejoice to no end.

It's then that I realize that *'inner struggles'* cease when *God's will* is carried out.

Upon me reaching my seat, Rev. Reeves states, "The Lord works in mysterious ways," in a surprisingly hushed manner.

Rev. Reeves isn't howling. Just the opposite—he's calm right now.

His calmness; a surprise to me . . . and probably, a surprise to everyone else in here.

The weird feeling I'd been harboring in my stomach has completely left.

Gone away.

Removed forever I feel.

It ended immediately after I'd laid the tray full of fans down.

Now, I am set free of my burden.

I never did make direct eye contact with Rev. Reeves while approaching him.

Why?

Well, truthfully speaking, what I figured is that *Rev. Reeves* wasn't *the person* who I had **to ultimately *'face-up to'*** concerning my issue.

You see, I know now, and without a doubt, that I, too, had come ***'face-to-face with God'***, in my struggle to overcome my wrongdoing.

Aunt Gayla still hasn't spoken a word to me since I've sat back down next to her.

Amazed, she sits next to me incapable of speaking—obviously welled-up with emotions.

I don't mention a word to her, either.

Her only actions are to alternate between wiping each eye. Besides this, she'll take peaks at the fan tray and Rev. Reeves.

I just heard Bro. Campbell, give three amens in a row; something he's never done before.

If my eyes aren't deceiving me, Rev. Reeves is actually trying to hold back tears.

He sits down to the left of the pulpit with his hand covering his whole face . . . all slumped over with both elbows resting in his lap.

"Why the left side of the pulpit? He has never sat on that side before." I notice in while continuing to survey his actions.

He lifts one finger. He gazes at the fan tray in apparent admiration.

Did he sit on the other side of the pulpit because he wanted to get a better view of me? Did he sit there because he wanted a better view at what lay before the pulpit?

Or . . .

Or, to be near O'Peniel's guardian angel . . .

I don't know. Only God knows.

Sis. Bradley continues to play the organ.

All caught-up in her own spirit of belief, her long notes sound like those you'd only hear in a mystery movie.

In time, church eventually dismisses.

Aunt Gayla has pretty much used an entire mini-pack of tissue.

No one in here dares to get up.

Or, to even approach Aunt Gayla or me.

"Perhaps, because . . ."

"Well, maybe . . ."

". . . I don't know why they haven't."

Anyhow, all members have remained seated.

Baffled is how the members come across to me.

Captivated; as if Jesus had just performed one of His miracles out of the bible.

Yea! That's how they seem right now. Quite fascinated by that fan tray ordeal, alright!

Mama always says my mind wonders too much.

Uncle Sherman sends Khoi back to where we're sitting in order for us to return to the hospital altogether. Heading this way, my brother is the first person to make any obvious moves in church.

First, he moves his eyeballs as far left as they'll go—to focus on me. Still stunned, he pushes his eyeballs to the lower right corner of his head. This time to quickly look at the fan tray. Finally, he, sits one pew away from Aunt Gayla and I.

Even though church members' weary eyes keep bouncing from the fan tray toward me, I know, *therefore, but by the grace of God*, I'd chosen to take the correct path!

After all, having hidden those fans back months ago had eaten away at my *conscious* for too long now.

CHAPTER 47

Revelations

During the ride back to see mama, Aunt Gayla resorts to using her finger tips to wipe away her tears. All of her tissue is now gone.

Words go unspoken in the car. Aunt Gayla takes a short-cut through the back of our neighborhood. Khoi doesn't bulge until we pass our house.

Looking toward it, he springs to the edge of the backseat and doesn't return to his former sitting position until he spots his football lying in the yard.

I, nonetheless, am still wondering why Aunt Gayla continues to cry since church is already over.

Mama's hanging up the phone when we arrive back at her room. She lies there looking more alert despite all of her pain.

She ignores the tubes attached to her arms and reaches for Khoi and me. Next, mama pulls her oxygen mask down under her chin.

"Come here both of you," She says, wearing a crisp, yellow hospital gown.

Visibly fragile, mama then gives us a lesser version of *'Kisses and Hugs Time'*.

Aunt Gayla, with her eyes still swollen, quickly walks out of the room.

She heads straight to the nurse's stand to get more tissue.

After returning, she signals for Grandmommy to follow her on the way back out.

Knowing my Aunt Gayla, she's probably informing her of my deed at church.

Mama turns her entire body in my direction.

"I just spoke with your Uncle Sherman. He tells me you came forward in church today with the missing fans."

Khoi shakes his head—'yes' without any hesitation—and before I could even answer for myself.

"Yes, ma'am," I finally reply.

"Rhyah Ann, you know O'Peniel had been looking for those fans for some time now.

We had thought that the new cleaning lady might have moved them by accident.

But, it was you!

You have caused such a great stir!"

"What's a stir?" I interrupt to ask.

"CONFUSION, Rhyah!

Confusion is what it means!"

Then, she comes back with, "What you have done is wrong!

Do you understand me? You are such a 'busy-body'!

You cannot bother things that don't belong to you.

What made you do such a thing, ANYWAY?"

Having already been eavesdropping, Aunt Gayla and Grandmommy quickly re-enter the room curiously awaiting my response.

"I just wanted to see what would happen if I *misplaced* the fans for a while.

It was warmer when I hid the fan tray. I knew no one would be using *'it'* for a while, at least."

"What is *it*?" mama returns to ask.

"*The coat closet*," I softly mumble not knowing what reaction I'd receive next.

Mama pushes the silver rack further away from her as if it's somehow blocking her view or not allowing her to hear me clearly.

Sprouting up slightly higher, "THE COAT CLOSET?" she confirms while racing to get her words out.

"Yes, ma'am."

"Huh?"

"Yes, ma'am, the coat closet is where I had hid the fan tray.

It was the day in which you told me to go and put those boxes in the storage room."

"On 'Children's Day', you mean?

Is this the day you're speaking of?" she questions seeking extra clarification.

Tears begin to roll and consequently fall from my cheeks.

Aunt Gayla hands me a wad of tissue that she'd been using for herself.

A short spell of silence is interrupted when a staff worker pages an emergency room doctor over the loud speaker. Following this, three paramedics rush by with a man bleeding on a stretcher.

Unsure of what to expect next, I go on to explain that, "There seems to be so many secrets being carried around in this world that people feel they have to live their lives *in—shame.* Even to the point, they'll harbor the pain behind **cover-ups**; *in this case, one of O'Peniel's church fans."*

"Cover-ups?

Church fans?

Rhyah Ann!

What?

What on God's green Earth are you speaking of?" mama squints her eyes to ask.

". . . and . . . and . . . all for what?" I exhale while continuing to speak.

"Mama, that shouldn't be. But, it seems that people will put forth great time and effort to do so. I don't want to be *'that person'* who has to tiptoe around town fearing what someone else may know or think about me.

It's like . . . umm . . . (I attempt to say with deep breaths taken) . . . it seems like the same things that make us glad in life can also take a turn to make us sad, too.

You see, mama, at church; it appears as though O'Peniel's members use those church fans to cover up *something* they might be *guilty of.*

Or, to otherwise use 'em to cover up *something* that they may want to remain *'a secret'.* Those fans aren't being used to help circulate the air, mama.

Plus, people with similar *secrets or sins* often appear to make others feel bad about their tribulations. When indeed, they in fact, have experienced or are struggling with the same concern.

*Mama, doesn't God forgive everyone-all the time, if you **earnestly** ask Him to with a **fervent heart?***"

My eyes flash away from mama momentarily to look over at Grandmommy. I'm hoping for a confirmation about my last question to mama. Instead, Grandmommy doesn't answer or even react; she just sits there lost for words as is everyone else.

"Mama . . . and . . . and since God forgives us, then why don't people do the same?

Nobody's perfect, mama!

NO ONE!

Not even Rev. Reeves.

This is all I was trying to say when I removed the fans from the storage room."

All eyes are still set upon me as I look down at my feet—remembering how these same feet guided me on the path at releasing my burden.

Wet from my tears, my tightly clasped hands are now shaking. I can almost hear my heart thumping away in my ears—because at this point, I can surely feel it.

With added confidence, I gradually step closer to mama and whisper, "Yes, it was wrong of me to have hidden the fans, but God sent my **guardian angel** *again* today to tell **me** to put the fan tray back."

Mama uses the side buttons to completely raise her bed up. She amazingly looks at Aunt Gayla with no apparent understanding of what I've just told her. Aunt Gayla, not wanting to miss out on anything, immediately comes to stand alongside me.

Resting near the foot of mama's hospital bed is Grandmommy. She even leans-in closer, causing it to shift somewhat.

Mama turns her weak body again. This time just to better affix her glossy eyes upon me.

She also twitches her body causing her hospital gown to slip off her erect shoulders.

"Who?

Gripping the gown along its seams, "Wha . . . , Wha . . . , What about this angel, Rhyah Ann?" she snips. Khoi, sitting in a chair watching a football game, spins around expecting an explanation, as well.

Ignoring mama's appeal for details concerning *the angel*, I, indeed, only choose to sum up what has been the basis for this all the while:

> *"You see, I do not want to have to walk around feeling ashamed when I get older; simply holding on to rotten memories in life. Nor, have sins that someday turn into haunting memories. Mama, I could have placed the fan tray back into the storage room where it belonged . . . and no one would have known it had been missing because of me . . . Ya know, 'throw the rock and then hide your hand'. Instead, I decided to place the fan tray down in front of all O'Peniel's members, as well as Rev. Reeves, too, today; letting everyone know that it was **I** who'd taken the fan tray and that we all make mistakes in life! In other words, I repented today, mama. . . . And all of this done without using a cover-up, either."*

"Well!" is all mama has to say, once I'd finished emptying out my heart to her. Aunt Gayla tries to speak but can't because her eyes are filling up with water again. Grandmommy remains quiet, too, until she sympathetically states,

> *"Vanessa, let bygones—be bygones.*
> *We've all had to bear 'that' cross.*
> *We've all had to wear 'that' crown, too.*
> *Remember GOD's servant, Job?*
> *. . . And at least, Vanessa, her heart was in the right*
> *place—and GOD surely read it.*
> *Her conscious is clear now.*
> *Now, let's just all be still and know that GOD is at work.*

Based upon Grandmommy's expressions, mama returns to her previous resting state. But, she continues to 'off again—on again' look my way. First, she'll peer up at the television then; re-shift her eyes straining to look back toward me. I guess she's trying to come to some sorta understanding about who my guardian angel is.

By now, my tears have ceased running down my pitiful face.

A nurse comes in to check some numbers on one of the bags that's attached to mama's silver rack.

Then, she jots something down on the chart before leaving.

The only continuous sounds in here are coming from the TV.

Apparently, mama can no longer hold her peace.

She breaks the quiet atmosphere to declare, "Rhyah Ann, all of that was not for you to be worrying about!

"It was for the Lord!" she exclaims pushing her finger up toward the ceiling.

"On the whole, I am proud of you for having returned the fan tray, but there's a lesson to be learned here.

The name of it is: 'A bought lesson is more important than a taught lesson!'"

After another quiet spell, she sneaks-in *'a little smile'* one that seems to light up those brown eyes of hers. Her cunning expression is one that I've never seen come across mama's face.

A different kinda smile, though—one that made me gleam back at her.

. . . and one that was only meant for me to see.

I guess she's more than just proud of me.

After having given this matter some thought, mama probably agrees with my reasons for having hidden the fans in the first place, is what I gather.

Another quiet session resumes.

A much longer one this time, though.

Although no one's venturing to speak out loud, silent words projected by silent thoughts fill the still air within mama's room.

Laughter in the hallway breaks this all up . . . yelping . . . and howling . . . some loud whistling, too. You'da thought a Second Line was approaching.

A male hospital worker enters mama's room carrying her food tray while blushing. He's grinning with his mouth closed—so hard that his cheeks are touching his eyes. I later learn Grandmommy's twin sisters had been making comments pertaining to him before he'd entered.

In walks Aunt Lorice, Aunt Jan and Aunt Norice. Gabriel trails in last.

The hospital worker is a young-looking man who appears to not be too much older than a teenager. He's wearing a baggy pair of blue uniform pants and his oversized shirt is not tucked in. He brings mama a small cup of peanut butter, three packages of crackers, two individually covered bowls, and a glass of cranberry juice with a cherry in it.

Raw carrots and cooked beets are in each of the covered bowls.

The outbursts of laughter from my great aunts get louder as the young man bends over to set-up mama's tray. Aunt Lorice makes eyes at the young man and teases him about being so cute. But, she makes sure to tell him that he's just too young for her hot Creole spices. "If you were just a little bit older . . . ," she finally allows him to hear her say as he exits the room.

Aunt Gayla leaves again. She takes charge of finding more chairs.

Everyone begins to greet one another. The level of noise in mama's small room rises.

Aunt Jan quietly informs mama that *I've been given my wings to fly* during their long, emotional hug. I don't know exactly what that means, but I assume it must have something to do with me *growing up*.

"Where's Leon?" Grandmommy inquires. Aunt Jan explains that he couldn't make it to the hospital. He went straight home following church service to explore future investment possibilities over the Internet.

It seems that after church, he and another deacon had discussed some sort of new stock opportunities. Uncle Leon, eager and not ever wanting to be outdone, went directly home to possibly readjust his own investment . . . ummm . . . port . . . porto . . . portofolo, I think it was called.

Amongst all the greetings, laughs and hugs, mama finishes eating everything on her tray, except the carrots.

Khoi ate 'em.

With a scrunched-up face, "Gross!" I kept saying to myself.

He kept flipping those carrots in his mouth like peanuts. Careless as he is, most of 'em ended up on the floor, anyway.

Oh!

And I nearly forgot. She didn't get to eat her cherry, either.

I snagged it while she was distracted hugging someone.

Uncle Sherman arrives with Aunt Margie.

Yes, . . . with Aunt Margie.

Apparently, he waited until she'd gotten off of work so they could come together.

"Hmmm. This is different!" I think to myself seeing her follow behind him.

I didn't think she cared enough to even show her face around all of us again.

I'm just glad; however, her kids didn't show up with 'em.

That would surely be torturous!

Morgan and Kristi eyeing me down . . .

Marcus and Paul, Jr. mocking me . . .

Not only that, but we'd all be packed in here like sardines, for sure!

A different nurse enters to recheck the levels on mama's medicine bags.

She also checks to see that mama's comfortable.

This time, no information is recorded on her chart. There are so many people in here; she probably forgot to do so.

Before attempting to leave, the nurse gets mama's food tray and removes the tray stand. She navigates the stand around mama's hospital bed and guides it around most everyone's legs similar to the way Aunt Gayla drives.

As a result, everyone has to shift for her convenience—causing a temporary chaos in this little room.

All of the chairs are occupied and no additional ones can fit.

Grandmommy and I already have to sit at the edge of mama's bed near her feet due to the lack of space.

I really can't tell where mama's feet stop because of the thick blankets lying on top of her.

She hasn't been transferred up stairs to a regular room yet.

So, everyone has to stuff themselves in here until they do finally schedule her move.

Under these crowded conditions, Aunt Margie is almost forced to talk to my family. As a matter of fact, numerous conversations are already taking place.

On the opposite side of the room, I notice Aunt Margie actively involved in a conversation with Aunt Norice. I guess there's no way anyone can act shy around my talkative family.

In another conversation, Aunt Gayla mentions she's decided to return to school in order to work on yet another degree. She and Aunt Jan are discussing her current educational plan when Aunt Lorice bursts into their conversation.

"Oh, boy!" she jumps in to interrupt them.

"Gayla Marie", she bats her false eye lashes to jokingly suggest, "you should save *THAT* money and accompany me on a singles cruise next summer!"

Every one laughs.

Even Aunt Margie giggles a bit.

Although it is stuffy in here, different discussions continue to ramble on.

Presently, I hear Aunt Margie describing to mama the number of orders the grocery store's bakery must fill on certain days. "Not to mention, if there are special orders to be filled on top of that."

Aunt Jan eavesdropping, as I am, interrupts to state, "That's called 'supply and demand'!" In return, Aunt Margie gives Aunt Jan a look of confusion which ends that conversation.

Gabriel, my Uncle Sherman, and Khoi are watching a football game.

With limited space, they've had to opt to standing. Cheering and making their own play-calls, they stand side by side. So close, it's not hard at all for each one to reach the other in order to give 'high-fives'. They're as excited as the football fans in the stadium. Barely able to move, Grandmommy manages to slightly turn toward 'em. "Don't forget we are in a hospital," she softly says with a fingertip placed over her lips.

"Lois Ann, before I forget, what do you think about this . . . ?" Aunt Norice breaks-in getting my Grandmommy's attention.

"We need to start making plans to attend our upcoming family reunion. This year, it's going to be in Texas sometime in the late spring. Do ya'll want to rent a 12-passenger van or drive our own cars? And, Lois Ann, we'll need to decide on how many days we'll need for reserving hotel rooms?" With so many conversations being held, Grandmommy just nods her head in acknowledgement without making a sound.

It sort of sounds like Ms. Carolyn's house in here; only with people instead of her dogs.

Thinking of Ms. Carolyn, I'm surprised she's not here!

"Mama!" "Mama! Where's Ms. Carolyn?"

Her head remains turned in the direction of another discussion. "Mamaaaaa!"

Unable to hear me, she continues to listen-in on my other relatives talking.

I wiggle the blankets to find her toes.

Startled!—She jumps and promptly turns to look toward the foot of her bed.

I then wave my hands to get her to notice that I'm the one seeking her attention.

With all the commotion, I just about have to scream, "W-h-e-r-e's M-s. C-a-r-o-l-y-n? I'm s-u-r-p-r-i-s-e-d s-h-e's n-o-t u-p h-e-r-e."

Mama is forced to answer back in the same manner. With a warped body position, a stretched-out neck, I make out that she said, "Ms. Carolyn called while we were all at church. And she'll be coming up after she finishes cooking."

Or, did mama say, "After stopping somewhere to pick up food." I am not sure.

I couldn't really understand at the end, but I know that Ms. Carolyn will absolutely be coming up here. She'll show up come rain or shine.

She's very supportive of mama. I guess you can pretty much say she's like a godmother to my brother and I. I'm also pretty sure she was one of the first persons Aunt Gayla contacted earlier, too.

The main discussion now turns to the recent championship game won by Khoi's football team. Mama's planning to host a big celebration party at our house for his whole team. Someone mentions whether or not my daddy will show up, especially since my brother was one of the team's key players.

"Probably not," I complain to myself.

The way I feel is that daddy didn't even come to any of his games; so why bother now.

Mama's big window in her room draws my attention away from everyone else at this point. Like always, my eyes and thoughts are roaming.

I squeeze by almost everyone to move toward the window.

Through the wide pane, I see plenty of people coming and going from this hospital.

A lady holding two children's hands while crossing the street, also, catches my eye.

The lady and her two kids remind me of our family portrait.

A city bus passes carrying a mass of people in it.

Two people exit the crowded bus, but the rest stay put awaiting their own destinations.

"Where are all of these people going?"

"I dunno."

"To live their lives," I casually assume.

I catch a better glimpse of the two ladies who've just exited the bus.

They're hurrying across the street.

The sight of 'em eventually gets blocked because of a tree.

A large tree.

A large magnolia tree that's also full of thick leaves that appear forever green.

It stands just to the right of mama's window.

It was probably here before this hospital was ever built. Why I say this: because it's full-sized roots are popping out of the ground.

Several different types of birds are moving around in it—actively leaping from branch to branch chirping at one another.

He he. It's funny, I can't understand what they're saying to one another, but God sure can.

Some fly away, but most remain with their flocks.

Hmmm.

I just realized something . . .

Birds have something in common with angels—wings to soar with.

Unexpectedly, a red bird circles the entire tree and then flies directly in front of this window. With a bright, red body and a head of the same deeper color, the bird soars gracefully away.

I push the left curtain back as far as it can go in order to follow its flight.

The red bird's velvety wings glide perfectly; all evenly stretched out on both sides.

With my hands still pressed against the glass window . . . I go on to wonder.

I haven't seen a red bird in a long time,"

Papa Joseph once told me that red birds were special.

He added that they're sent directly from Heaven to pass on *God's most special messages* and this is why we don't see too many of 'em.

"Could this red bird have been mama's guardian angel in some form? Flying near her room to check on her?" I suspect, thinking about my own guardian angel.

Papa Joseph also taught me that if you complete a wish before a red bird leaves your sight, your wish would someday come true.

With my face now pressed against the window, "Where's it going now?" I try to figure out. "I have no idea, but I guess . . . just going about its business passing on God's messages from Heaven."

Khoi and I are staying at Grandmommy's house until mama's released from the hospital. She was finally moved upstairs to her own private room. I don't think Grandmommy was going to leave her side until they had done so. Her chest x-rays did show a few deficiencies, but that's o.k. That was to be expected, anyway, as noted by one of the nurses. Oh, yea! And mama finally received a pair of socks. It wasn't until my Aunt Gayla went to the nurse's station to request 'em that they finally arrived. I can only wonder what she said to those nurses.

I felt bad for mama and all, but I was starting to get tired of seeing those nurses coming in and out . . . out and in . . . and then, in and back out again to either to adjust the bags on her silver rack or to ask her questions. Other than that, just to check on her.

Whew! Gosh, those nurses ask more questions than Aunt Gayla does, especially the one with the foreign accent! That particular nurse came on duty before we left the hospital. She carefully went over mama's chart line-by-line; only stopping long enough to receive short answers from mama.

At one point, I began to imagine if that's how I carry on at times. Because, I'd hate to grow up and be just like Aunt Gayla—constantly throwing question after question to people. Mama says I do ask a lot of questions, though. My teachers tell her I do this at school, too. I know this probably gets on my teacher's nerves, because it surely gets on mama's. Not giving people time to answer is possibly another issue I have. I know I can get pretty detailed, but I just want to always know the full story.

I asked Grandmommy as we were preparing to leave the hospital if I did indeed asked a lot of questions.

In complete silence and reaching for my hand, she only smiled at me.

On the whole, I pat my own self on the back.

Why?

Well, I just want to be able to *sort things* out in life; as they apply to me.

But, mostly to see how matters of life *fit into* or *affect 'my world'*.

After leaving the hospital, we stopped by our house to get enough clothes to last at least a week. We took our backpacks for the upcoming week at school.

Everything else we needed is already here at Grandmommy's house.

Stuff like: spare toothbrushes, extra socks, emergency sets of underclothes, and even some spare p.j.'s.

Khoi made sure to grab his football along with his little, blue night-light.

Besides my clothes, I couldn't forget my diary or my dictionary that lay beside it. Oh! . . . and before Grandmommy locked our front door, I ran back in to get my bucket of hair bows.

Grandmommy, herself, had to gather a few items, to be taken back to mama on tomorrow. On the way to mama's bedroom, Grandmommy stopped to fluff some sofa pillows in our living room. Pausing for only a moment, she stopped to straighten our family portrait. I watched as she moved it around trying to seek a 'perfect' spot for it.

I asked Grandmommy could we take the portrait back to mama's hospital room tomorrow; in hopes that this might make her feel more at home.

Overall, Grandmommy agreed with my suggestion, but concluded that we'd just take it to her house, instead.

Before I could ask her, "Why so?" she went on to explain that having the portrait at her house would be more like having everyone at home still. I guess Grandmommy probably figured my brother and I needed the portrait around us, more so than mama having it up there at the hospital.

For the most part, every time we stay with Grandmommy, I tend to sleep in mama's ol' room. Her cream-colored walls are starting to fade, but they allow me to easily lose myself while daydreaming. There is one thing that I don't like about this room, though. This ol' box spring squeaks letting Grandmommy know when I'm up and about when I'm supposed to be asleep.

As for Khoi, he always chooses to sleep in Uncle Sherman's ol' room. It's the one nearest Grandmommy's back porch. A couple of autographed sports pictures hang above the rod iron headboard. Another picture of Uncle Sherman participating in a rodeo back in high school hangs near the dresser. Uncle Sherman's ol' room also remains in the same bold colors he once had it in.

. . . And as for Aunt Gayla's ol' room—neither one of us *ever* choose to sleep in there.

Before Grandmommy tucked me in tonight, I finally finished writing my last diary entry.

I'm glad, too.

Because she's turned off every light in the house.

Except for one; Khoi's night-light.

She pulled the covers all the way up to my chin while commenting on this evening's chilly forecast.

Next, she walked around this entire bed making sure its sheets fit tightly.

I could barely move then and as for now, my position hasn't changed.

Like a cocoon: I remain trapped under these heavy covers.

. . . And I too, as always, said my prayers.

Due to being tucked in so firmly, I had to remain in bed reciting 'em in the same snug position she'd left me lying in.

Rhyah's Diary Entry Tonight:

Today was a very busy day for me. I learned a lot. Especially, that life is full of struggles. It's often a gamble. Better yet, it is a game that comes with no instructions. So, during the times of war and peace in my life, I must listen to my heart (the dwelling place of my guardian angel). Its only then, that I won't be misled. I know, because my guardian angel showed me this today.

Rhyah

Rhyah's Prayer Tonight:

"Dear God,

We all know life is full of surprises and lessons, too. I have figured it all out. It's kind of like You deal each of us (all) a hand of cards. It's only what we do with that hand that makes all the difference.

God, please, help me to always make the right choices in life.

Thank you for my Grandmommy.
And pleaseeee, take care of mama

. . . and daddy, too.

In Jesus' name.
Amen!"

"Oh, Yea!

Dear God,

Please remind my guardian angel to keep making those deals with that 'other' angel."

Kimberly N. Williams © 2003